KAYE UMANSKY

Wilma's Wicked SPELL

Illustrated by Tony Blundell

PUFFIN BOOKS

Published by the Penguin Group
Penguin Books Ltd, 80 Strand, London WC2R 0RL, England
Penguin Putnam Inc., 375 Hudson Street, New York, New York 10014, USA
Penguin Books Australia Ltd, 250 Camberwell Road, Camberwell, Victoria 3124, Australia
Penguin Books Canada Ltd, 10 Alcorn Avenue, Toronto, Ontario, Canada M4V 3B2
Penguin Books India (P) Ltd, 11 Community Centre, Panchsheel Park, New Delhi – 110 017, India
Penguin Books (NZ) Ltd, Cnr Rosedale and Airborne Roads, Albany, Auckland, New Zealand
Penguin Books (South Africa) (Pty) Ltd, 24 Sturdee Avenue, Rosebank 2196, South Africa

Penguin Books Ltd, Registered Offices: 80 Strand, London WC2R 0RL, England

www.penguin.com

First published 2002
1

Text copyright © Kaye Umansky, 2002
Illustrations copyright © Tony Blundell, 2002
All rights reserved

The moral right of the author and illustrator has been asserted

Set in Bembo

Made and printed in England by Clays Ltd, St Ives plc

British Library Cataloguing in Publication Data
A CIP catalogue record for this book is available from the British Library

ISBN 0–141–31013–8

CONTENTS

1. BREAKFAST

The letter from Great-Aunt Angria arrived one Tuesday morning and changed my life.

But wait, I hear you cry! What letter is this? Who is Great-Aunt Angria? What was your life like before anyway?

You're quite right. I'm ahead of myself. If I'm going to tell you this, I might as well do it properly. Let's move back and fill you in a little.

It was boring old breakfast-time one boring old Tuesday morning and we were all seated around the table eating boring old eggs. Well, when I say *all,* I mean just Mother, Daddy and me. Our family was rather depleted at this point in time. Everyone else was away enjoying themselves: Grandma, Aunt Maud, New Uncle

I

Frank, Cousin Alvis, Uncle Bacchus and both my horrible sisters, Frostia and Scarlettine. All off having new and exciting experiences and generally getting on with their lives. All except me. I wasn't going anywhere nice or doing anything remotely exciting and, quite frankly, I was fed up to the back teeth. I would have stayed in bed, but Mother always insists I get up for breakfast. It's the only time she gets to have a good old nag at me.

'Wilma,' said Mother, sharply, 'sit up and eat your egg properly.'

She was annoyed because I was still slobbing around in my dressing-gown and hadn't brushed my hair. She, of course, was all got up in her official black robes, glamorous as ever despite having just got back from the Round. She's the only person I know who wears evening gloves at breakfast.

(I should explain that Mother is the Queen of the Night. This might sound exotic, but actually it's a really hard job, involving nightly sick-making journeys around the globe at supernaturally high speed. That's what we call the Round, or Bringing the Night. She never gets a holiday. I don't know how she does it.)

'I don't want to eat my egg,' I said. 'I'm bored with my egg. That's why I'm resting my head on it.'

'Well, don't. Your hair is full of eggshell. I don't think you've brushed it for a week. I gave you that lovely new brush for your birthday and I don't think you've used it once.'

'Why bother?' I said. 'I'm not going anywhere. Anyway, I like eggshell in my hair. I'm making a statement.'

'Don't be cheeky, Wilma! I'm tired of you hanging about in that disgusting dressing-gown, being cheeky!'

'I'm only hanging about because there's nothing to do,' I pointed out reasonably. 'Why can't I go on holiday? Everyone else is.'

'Wilma, we've just bought you a very expensive guitar.'

'But you won't let me practise it! I've got to practise!'

'Not around us you don't. Practise in your room.'

'But I want you and Daddy to hear!'

'We *have* heard. We've heard your guitar playing a *lot*. And the fact remains that it cost a lot of money. You can't have everything.'

'I'm not asking for everything. Just a holiday would be fine.'

'Tell her, George,' said Mother tiredly. 'I really can't be bothered to deal with it this morning. I've got one of my heads coming on.'

I felt a bit guilty then. After all, she'd been working all night. It's no wonder she's never at her best first thing in the morning.

But then again, who is?

'Come on, Wilma,' said Daddy, glancing up from his gardening magazine. *Mulch Monthly*, I think it was. 'Sit up, pet, there's a dear.'

'Ahem, ahem.'

A polite little cough came from the doorway. That was Peevish our butler, grovelling around with the morning's post on a silver tray.

'Ah, the post!' Mother exclaimed, brightening. 'Bring it here, would you?'

3

Peevish approached the table with his usual servile crawl. I stuck out a surreptitious foot to trip him up, but he knows my little ways by now and avoided it. Furtively, I loaded up a spoonful of jam. I'd get him on the way back. OK, so it was a bit babyish. But I was bored, right?

'Thank you, Peevish,' said Mother, taking the pile from the silver platter. 'By the way, do tell Mrs Pudding that the eggs were *lovely*. Weren't they, George?'

'Mmm?' said Daddy, nose deep in compost.

'The eggs. Weren't they lovely?'

'Mmm.'

'Delicious,' said Mother firmly. 'Even better than usual, tell her. Then ask her if it would be at all possible to have just a *teensy* bit more toast? If she'd be so kind?'

'Regrettably, ma'am, she has put the loaf away,' sighed Peevish, oozing sorrow. 'It's the morning she visits her sister. The kitchen has been cleared and I fear she has her coat on. Of course, I could always *try* –'

'Oh, no, no, no, no, don't do *that*!' cried Mother hastily. 'Not if she's got her coat on.'

It doesn't do to upset our Mrs Pudding. Like most puddings, she has a tendency to boil over. It's worth remembering that cooks always have the upper hand because they can sneeze in the food. Not that Mrs Pudding has ever sneezed in *our* food, of course.

I think.

I hope.

But we never ever criticize and are always extra polite, just in case.

'She asked me to relay a message, ma'am,' warned

Peevish. He held out a piece of paper, obviously torn off a flour bag and scribbled on in high fury.

'Oh dear. Have I upset her in some way? What?'

'I'll read it, shall I, ma'am?'

'Yes, yes, *what*?'

Peevish held the note close to his eyes and read:

'*Ma'am. I'll thank you to keep Miss Wilma out of the kitchen. I can't stand another day of it.*'

'Well, thanks a lot,' I said, hurt. 'I was only trying to *help*.'

I thought I had been welcome in the kitchen, making chocolate cake and chocolate trifle and chocolate steak and kidney pudding and stuff and helpfully rearranging the pantry shelves using the simple system of putting all the things that I like best at the front. Well, it made sense to *me*. And it wasn't my fault, the thing that happened with the mincer.

'Stay out of the kitchen, Wilma,' said Mother. 'That's an order. Mrs Pudding has a job to do. She's not there for your amusement.'

'What am I *supposed* to do, then?' I demanded sniffily. 'Can't lie in, can't go anywhere, can't play my guitar, can't even *cook*. What?'

'Try doing some work for a change. You are supposed to be studying for your Grade Four Magic Certificate, are you not?'

'I know it all already,' I said. Well, I *did*. Grade Four is so easy a goblin could do it, and everyone knows how stupid *they* are. 'I could take the exam tomorrow if I'd done the work experience. You keep saying you'll arrange it, but you never do.'

This was true. Work experience with a qualified

Magical practitioner is an essential requirement of the Grade Four exam. Mother kept saying she'd sort something out but she never seemed to get round to it.

'Don't use that tone with me, Wilma,' snapped Mother. Her Aura was nearly black. (Did I mention she has an Aura? It comes with the job. It's a sort of dark glow surrounding her which reflects how she's feeling. A kind of mood indicator.) 'Don't you think I've got enough on my mind? What with Grandma going off to the Gypsy Convention with Maud and Frank in that *dreadful* little caravan and poor Frostia with her building problems and Scarlettine on the high seas.'

'And young Alvis,' added Daddy. 'He's taken the week off. *Gone fishin'* is what he told me. And me with a wagonload of mulch on its way and the Tomato of the Year Show coming up.'

'And Bacchus,' chipped in Mother. 'Don't forget him. He's *still* not answering his Ball. I've left three messages on it now. I've worries enough without your work experience, Wilma. If you're that keen, you could always organize it yourself, you know.'

I said nothing to that. Organizing my own work experience would mean getting out of bed and putting on clothes and writing endless grovelling letters and finding matching shoes so I could go to the post office for stamps. It was all too much like hard work. Far better to wait and let Mother do it for me. She has a big enough circle of friends. Surely *somebody* would take me on? Maybe Lady Luck would let me trail round after her for a couple of days. Or Mother's old friend the Storm Queen (privately referred to by me and Daddy as Rumbleguts).

Actually, I wouldn't mind working for Rumbleguts for a day or two. It would be good to learn the ins and outs of Storm Management. I particularly fancy having a go at a Storm in a Teacup, which apparently requires a very steady hand if you're not to electrocute yourself with all those miniature lightning-bolts.

But I'm going too fast again. I should fill you in a little, after that complicated speech by Mother. It's only fair to try and break it down into manageable chunks of information. There are things you need to know, and now is as good a time as any. So. Pin back your ears for a brief update on my mad family.

Grandma (Queen of the Night retired, former mad, sprout-eating tower-dweller) had recently undergone a belated personality change brought about by being reunited with her long-lost daughter, Maud (my aunt, Mother's sister, long hair, talks to trees, sings folksongs – you know the sort). I had a lot to do with them getting reunited, actually, but that's another story.

Aunt Maud has a husband – a silent type called Frank Parsley, who plays the flute. I call him New Uncle Frank. We've never actually spoken. Aunt Maud and New Uncle Frank had gone off to a Gypsy Convention, taking a pink-cheeked, overexcited Grandma with them. They said they were planning to *bond*, which I think means getting to know each other. Mother didn't think it wise, but you don't argue with Grandma, improved personality or not.

Alvis Parsley (son of Aunt Maud and New Uncle Frank, my cousin, helps Daddy in the garden, plays guitar) had taken Buster the dog and gone off into the wilds. He had also taken his guitar, his hair gel and some of Daddy's old gardening magazines.

My oldest sister, Frostia (Queen of the Snow, snooty, always wears white, thoroughly hateful), was up at the North Pole supervising the building of her new palace. The old one had been quite recently brought down by a combination of global warming and me, actually, but again that's another story.

My other sister, Scarlettine (Queen of Mirrors, well-known poisoner, show-off, always wears red, even worse than Frostia if that's possible), was currently on a luxury cruise, getting over her heartache at being exposed as the baddy in the Snow White affair. (I had also had my finger in *that* particular pie – but we won't go into it now.) She had bought a veil and dark glasses to give herself the air of a mystery woman. She hadn't even taken her Crystal Ball so no one could contact her even if they wanted to. She said she wanted to be alone.

Hah!

Uncle Bacchus (Mother's bachelor brother, god of wine or something, lives in a tumbledown castle on a scruffy island, eating takeaway kebabs) hadn't answered his Crystal Ball in over three days – but that wasn't unusual. Mother worries about him too much. He has a lot of meals with us because he doesn't know how to cook, although he's got no problem with eating or drinking, I notice.

That's enough about the family for now. Back to the breakfast table.

'Will that be all, Your Majesty?' enquired Peevish.

'Yes thank you, Peevish, you may go.'

Off he creaked, keeping well out of jam range, much to my sorrow. I put the spoon down and secretly started pocketing sugar lumps.

'Now then,' said Mother. 'Let's see what the post has brought. Bill, bill, function, function, bill, invitation to lunch at the Hall of the Mountain King, another function, cocktails with Cupid next Thursday, another bill – Aha!' With a happy little cry, she pounced. 'Look, George! It's a postcard from Scarlettine!'

'That's nice,' said Daddy. 'Read it out, then, dearest.'

'*Dear Mother and darlingest Daddy,*' read Mother. '*Having a lovely time. Wish you were here but glad Wilma isn't. Everyone on board is hopelessly in love with me. Tonight, I dine at the captain's table. He cannot take his eyes off me. What do you think? Do you see me as a captain's wife? Your loving daughter Scarlettine. P.S. Give Wilma a kick for me.*'

'Huh! Captain's wife, my foot,' I growled. 'Does he know about her reputation as a poisoner? He'll learn, when he tastes her fish soup.'

'Oh, do stop sounding so sour, Wilma,' sighed Mother. 'Here. This one's for you.' She handed me a card.

I took it and stared at it. There was a picture of a penguin in sunglasses on an iceberg. The message on the other side was WILMA. STAY COOL. ALVIS.

Great.

That was all, apart from another one of Daddy's boring gardening magazines. Or was it?

'Good gracious,' said Mother. 'Whatever's this?'

At the bottom of the pile, buried beneath *Tomato World*, was a large, square envelope with a black border. Mother picked it up gingerly and examined it at arm's length. It bore no stamp. It was addressed quite simply to *The Queen of the Night, Ancestral Halls* in heavy, black gothic writing. It looked different from the sort of junk one usually gets in the post. Important. Strange. *Sinister.*

'George,' said Mother slowly, turning it over in her gloved hand. 'See the crest? Starkacre Hall. You know what we have here, don't you?'

'I do indeed,' said Daddy. He had his head out of his magazine for once. He and Mother were exchanging meaningful glances.

'What?' I said, sensing something in the air. 'What is it?'

'Unless I am very much mistaken,' said Mother, 'what we have here is a letter from Aunt Angria.'

2. THE LETTER

Whooh! Surprise, surprise. Aunt Angria, eh? It had been a very long time since anyone had mentioned *her* name. She is Grandma's sister, which actually makes her my great-aunt.

To the rest of the world, she is known as the Thirteenth Faerie. (Note the spelling. Not Fairy. *Faerie*.)

'How long has it been, do you think, George,' asked Mother, slitting the envelope with the butter knife, 'since we last saw her in person?'

'On our wedding day,' said Daddy tightly. 'When she came storming down the aisle shrieking curses and making all the flowers wilt and the wine turn to vinegar.'

'I do believe you're right. Oh, George, now I feel terrible. I should have written to check on her.'

'Why?' said Daddy. 'She tried to ruin our wedding. The butter turned sour on all the cheesy biscuits. Our special day was quite spoiled.'

'Oh, darling. That's just her way. She is family, when all's said and done. And she's a *very* old lady now. She's probably retired. And she did have good reason to be cross with us. She claimed she never received the invitation.'

'Ah, but that's her stock-in-trade, isn't it? Pretending she doesn't get invited to things. It's just an excuse to allow her to – to *slam* into places and shoot off a lot of indiscriminate cursing. Your mother can be trying at times, but Angria's just plain *nasty*. Drop it in the bin, Veronica. No good will come of it.'

I must say I was quite surprised at all this, coming from Daddy. He's a peace-maker by nature. Great-Aunt Angria must be quite something to bring out all this bad feeling.

Mother patted his hand, then ignored him, as usual. She had removed a single sheet of paper from the envelope and was reading, with a pained little frown on her pale brow.

I mentally riffled through the dusty files of ancient family history which I carry in my head, trying to locate what I knew about my great-auntie. According to Grandma, as a child she was a vile-tempered little madam who never got invited to parties. Grandma, being the older of the two, inherited the coveted title of Queen of the Night. I gather that this didn't go down too well with Angria, who promptly stormed out of the Ancestral Halls and holed up in a place of her own, only ever emerging to burst into various functions to which she wasn't invited and curse everyone in sight. The original party pooper, in fact.

Her rather sinister title – the Thirteenth Faerie – came about because of a particular incident which happened years and years ago. She was involved in some sort of drama over a christening, a curse and a royal baby. I wasn't too sure of the details, but apparently some goody-goody Fairy humiliated her in public or something, after which she just dropped from view. Then, a few years later, there was an unpleasant incident at somebody or other's birthday party, but I'm not sure what. Nobody talks about it much. It's one of those grim secrets our family goes in for.

Of course, all this happened donkey's years ago. All right, so our family is immortal (did I mention this?) but nobody wants to carry on working for ever. Everyone assumed Great-Aunt Angria had retired. At any rate, she went ex-directory with her Crystal Ball and refused to answer the door to callers. Ten years ago she stopped sending Christmas cards and all communication ceased.

Until now.

'What does she want?' asked Daddy with a little sneer which was quite unlike him. 'Some sort of favour, I'll bet.'

'Well – yes,' admitted Mother. 'But, actually, this might suit us very well. Particularly you, Wilma. Listen. *So, Veronica. Another decade passes and none of ye has written the scrawl of a pen, let alone visited. But then, I don't expect it any more in these modern times when nobody can even be bothered to write a word of gratitude for monies sent.'* Mother broke off and gave a little sigh.

'What's that all about?' asked Daddy.

'She must be referring to that postal order for ten pence she sent years ago to Scarlettine on her eighth birthday. I didn't think you could even *get* postal orders for ten pence. Scarlettine never did write and thank her. Oh dear.'

'Carry on,' I said. I wanted to know what I was supposed to find so interesting in this moany old letter. 'What does she want?'

Mother returned to the letter.

'*Me, I prefer to stick with the olde ways, where youngsters respect their elders and betters and welcome the opportunity to give them a bit of help and maybe learn something.*

'*And so to business. I understand that your two eldest girls are now queens in their own right and doubtless too tied up with their own selfish affairs to do a mild favour for their great-aunt.*

'*I wasn't invited to your youngest girl's last birthday celebration, as ye might expect, but by my reckoning she will be twelve or thereabouts. I assume she is reasonably competent in the Magickal Arts –*'

'Huh,' I interrupted. 'Reasonably competent, my foot!' I passed my Grade Three Magic exam with honours, which isn't bad going for twelve. I'm more than reasonably competent. I'm *good*!

'Shush, Wilma. The next bit concerns you. *At this point in time I am engaged in an important, highly secret Magickal project and in urgent need of assistance. Normally I wouldn't ask, in fact I'd sooner walk on hot coals, but I have lately been* *suffering from gout, which **does** feel like walking on hot coals, not that anyone cares. Suffice to say, I'm finding it hard to get about.*

'*I don't know the name of your youngest girl. Not one of ye had the common courtesy to tell me and, needless to say, I got no invite to her christening. Anyway, be that as it may. If she proves up to the job, I shall require her for three full days. She will return on the night of Friday the thirteenth. Her board and lodging and all Magickal equipment will be provided. She might like to bring her own Wand.*

'*Bring her to Starkacre tonight (Tuesday the tenth). I shall be waiting.*

'*Angria, the Thirteenth Faerie.*

'*P.S. Are ye still married to that ridiculous little balding fellow who made such a fuss at the wedding?*'

'Well!' exclaimed Daddy. 'If that doesn't beat all!'

'Oh, I don't know,' said Mother. 'It is nice to hear from her again. We have rather neglected her. And it does sort out the problem of Wilma's work experience.'

'*What?*' Daddy almost shouted. 'You can't be serious! You'd send our Wilma along to learn at the knee of that – that *dreadful* old woman?'

'I don't see why not. At least it would stop her sitting around moaning that she never goes anywhere. You'd like to meet your Great-Aunt Angria, wouldn't you, Wilma? Get out of the Ancestral Halls for a few days? You can take your guitar and play it to her. It'd make a nice change for us. You, I mean.' She corrected herself hastily. 'A nice change for *you*. And Aunt Angria will enjoy the company, I'm sure. All by herself in that lonely old castle.'

'Maybe,' I said cautiously. It had all been rather sprung on me. I needed to think it over.

'I forbid it!' said Daddy. 'Wilma, you're not going, and that's final.'

'Now, George.' Mother reached over and patted his knee. 'This is wicked queen business. Leave it to me, there's a dear. Shouldn't you be tending your tomatoes?'

'I don't know.' Poor Daddy stood up, shaking his head. 'Myself, I feel that the last thing Wilma needs is Magic lessons from a homicidal maniac, but who am I?'

'Absolutely. Have a lovely morning, darling.'

Dejectedly, Daddy wandered out in the direction of the garden.

'So,' said Mother, stifling a yawn. I could see she was dying to get to bed. 'What about it, Wilma? I could drop you off tonight when I'm doing the Round. What do you say?'

Well, now cooking was out, there was nothing else exciting on the horizon. And I must admit I was intrigued.

'All right,' I said, with a shrug. 'Why not?'

3. THE JOURNEY

'Nervous, darling?' asked Mother.

'Who, me? Certainly not,' I said. Well, I wasn't. It takes more than an antique great-auntie to put the wind up me. 'Should I be?'

'Oh, no,' said Mother. 'I have every confidence in you, Wilma. I'm sure you will cope admirably.'

We were sitting in the Night Coach, waiting for the last rays of the setting sun to sink below the horizon. The Night Coach is the official conveyance used by Mother on the Round. It's an all-black affair, with tinted windows and black plumes waving at each corner. It's pulled by two wild-eyed, evil-tempered black horses called Clint and Horace, who consider themselves a cut above average horses just because they can fly.

My trunk was stored on the roof and Muckbucket, the head groom, was already in the driver's seat, preparing to set off. I confess I wasn't looking forward to the journey. I hate Bringing the Night. Circling the globe at heights where eagles dare not go, swooping along ten times faster than a speeding arrow, all those tummy-churning inter-dimensional hyper-leaps. Uggh.

There came the sound of Muckbucket shouting his usual calm, loving words of encouragement to the horses.

'Gercha, yer blinkin' animals, gidalongthere, lor' love a duck, get yer flamin' fat backsides *up*, will ya!'

The whip cracked and the coach jerked forward, gravel crunching under the wheels. We gradually gained speed until we were hurtling down the drive on collision course with the fast-approaching gates, which were firmly closed. Then, just as I was bracing myself for the crash, we were tipped abruptly backwards as Clint and Horace leaped for the sky and the front wheels left the ground.

I closed my eyes and reached for the sick bag. When I opened them again, we were airborne.

'Peppermint?' said Mother, holding out a bag with an amused little smile.

'Blurk. Thanks,' I said, and took three. I risked a quick glance out of the tinted window. There was nothing below but a sea of dark clouds edged with moonlight. A shadowy jet stream of silken blackness unfurled in our wake, spreading and curling and drifting wide as we left it behind. Little stars twinkled in it. That was the Night, of course, and we were Bringing It.

I turned back from the window, sucked vigorously on the peppermints and stared at the roof to steady myself.

'Relax, Wilma,' said Mother. 'Sit back. Enjoy the ride. It's not often we spend quality time together. I'm your mother. Talk to me. Tell me all your little girlish problems. Is there anything you'd like to discuss, now we're all quiet and on our own?'

'Well, there's the question of my pocket money,' I said, seizing the moment. 'I thought you said I'd get a raise when I was twelve? My birthday was ages ago, and I'm still only getting –'

'On second thoughts, perhaps we'll just sit quietly,' interrupted Mother.

'But I'm only getting –'

'Enough!'

Her Aura was darkening. I subsided. She leaned back, smoothing a wrinkle in the black velvet travelling-rug that lay across her knees.

'I hope you've packed sensible things in your trunk,' she said.

'Oh, I have,' I said. Well, I had. This is what I put in:

Three packets of chocolate biscuits
My Grade Three (with honours) Magic Certificate
My Wand
My guitar
Graham, my stuffed frog, who I sometimes sleep
*   with*
A bag of doughnuts
Some sugar lumps
My new MoBall (like a Crystal Ball, but pocket-
*   sized)*
A hot-water bottle

A box of chocolate eclairs
A box of individually wrapped mince pies
A box of Magic Candles
Denzil, Mrs Pudding's cat

Denzil was a last-minute addition. He got into the trunk when I was packing and started kneading the stuffing out of Graham. He then settled down on the hot-water bottle and drooled. He looked so comfortable, I didn't have the heart to disturb him. So I just punched a few air holes in the lid and said nothing. Denzil would have a lovely holiday and it would pay back Mrs Pudding for complaining about me to Mother.

'I hope you've packed your hairbrush,' continued Mother. 'And that nice new pretty blue dress I bought you. And something to sleep in, and soap and shampoo. And your toothbrush. And warm vests. I've never visited Starkacre Hall myself, but knowing Great-Aunt Angria's style, it's sure to be chilly. Did you remember your hot-water bottle?'

'Of course,' I said with cold scorn, seizing on the one thing she had mentioned that I *had* included. 'I'm not *that* stupid. Give me *some* credit.'

'Of course I do, darling.' Mother gave me a tired little smile. 'I keep forgetting that you're not a little girl any more. Why, it won't be many more years before you're a wicked queen in your own right, with a castle of your own, like your sisters. Just think. My little Wilma, off on her own for three whole days, doing real work experience. This is a wonderful opportunity, you know. Aunt Angria had quite a reputation in her day. She knows her stuff. Of course, she'll only be *dabbling* in Magic now, in a pottery, part-time, senior citizenish sort of way, but I'm sure you'll learn a lot.'

'Ah, yes. Her reputation,' I said, glad to steer the conversation away from the subject of packing. 'What's that all about, then? Wasn't there some sort of scandal involving a baby or something?'

'Not exactly a *scandal*. More a sort of mildly embarrassing incident. Some people felt she went a little over the top, that's all. But it was just her way. Hold on, Wilma. First leap coming up.'

I gritted my teeth and grabbed hold of the leather strap that hung from the roof. The coach gave a violent lurch and my tummy tried to jump out through my throat. Outside the window, there was a blinding flash of light, and a fleeting impression of spiralling stars rushing towards us. Then another bump, and we were back as before, flying smoothly over a new set of clouds with the Night unravelling behind us.

'That wasn't too bad, was it?' said Mother brightly. 'Only another three to go.'

I didn't reply because I was choking on the peppermints. From over our heads came the unmistakable sound of an annoyed cat which has awoken from sleep only to find itself trapped in a trunk undergoing an inter-dimensional hyper-leap with not a fish head in sight.

'What was that?' enquired Mother, leaning over to pat me on the back.

'What?' I gasped, spitting out bits of mashed mint.

'Funnily enough, I thought I heard a cat cry.'

'Did you? I thought it was a horse snorting. Clint, probably. I've often noticed his snort has a sort of cat-like sound. But you were saying?'

'I was just saying that Great-Auntie had a certain old-fashioned way of doing things that wasn't to everyone's liking. She belongs to the fire and brimstone school. She doesn't approve of contemporary Magical thinking. Too subtle. She just lets fly.'

'Like Grandma?' I asked. Grandma's not too fussy who she zaps with her Magic Stick when she's in one of her moods. Of course, she makes out she's all sweetness and light these days, since the return of her prodigal daughter, but *I'm* not deceived.

'Worse,' said Mother, adding, 'But she's a very old lady now. I'm sure she's mellowed.'

'She didn't sound very mellow in her letter,' I remarked.

'Oh, that's just her way,' said Mother. 'Anyway, I'm sure you'll get used to her. My only worry is, will she get used to you?'

'What's that supposed to mean?' I asked.

'Nothing, darling, nothing. I'm sure she'll learn to love you in time, just like we did. We're going to miss you, you know, Daddy and I.'

'It's only three days,' I pointed out. 'I'll be back on Friday.'

'Even so, it'll seem strange, not having you drooping around the place. I hope you won't feel lonely when you go to bed tonight without a story or a lullaby.'

'You've never told me a story or sung me a lullaby,' I told her. 'I'll get by.'

'Oh?' Mother looked vaguely surprised. 'Haven't I? *Really*, darling? I'm sure I did with the other two.'

'Not me, though,' I said, putting a pitiful little wobble into my voice. Well, it's true. She's always out on the Round when I go to bed.

'Ah me,' sighed Mother. 'What a neglectful mother I am. The sacrifices one has to make to hold down a career. Still, we're making up for it now, aren't we? All cosy together. Shall I tell you a bedtime story now, hmm? You're not too big, are you? Hmm? How about *The Phantom Face at the Window*? Your sisters always loved that. How they used to scream!' She chuckled fondly at the memory.

'No thanks,' I said. Well, I'd heard it a million times already. My sisters always took great pleasure in scaring me silly with it at bedtime. That was when I was little, of course. I've toughened up since then. Well, I've had to.

'What about a lullaby, then? What was that one I always used to sing to the girls? Something about a Goblin.'

'You mean "There's a Child-Gobbling Goblin Under the Bed"?' I knew it well. Frostia and Scarlettine used to serenade me with it every night.

'That's it! How did it go again?' Mother hummed a bar or two in a rich, wobbly contralto, then burst into song.

'There's a child-gobbling Goblin lives under the bed,
  Lullay, lullay,
His teeth are brass and his eyes are red,
  Lullay, lullay,
He's sure to come out when the lights are off,
  Lullay, lullay,
With his sharp green teeth and his terrible cough ...'

'*Enough!*' I cried. 'Honestly, Mother, it really isn't necessary, OK?'

'All right,' said Mother, sounding a bit hurt. 'I was just trying to cheer you up, darling.'

'I know. But don't. I'd rather know about the embarrassing incident. Why is Great-Aunt Angria known as the Thirteenth Faerie? Who are the other twelve?'

'I really can't remember the details now, Wilma. It all happened a long time ago. Water under the bridge. Let's talk about something else, shall we? I hope you've packed your new MoBall? I wouldn't like to feel I couldn't get in touch with you.'

'Of course,' I said scornfully. As if I'd leave *that* behind. It's my lifeline to the normal world. Well, in my case, the world's never exactly *normal*, but you know what I mean. 'I'll flash you later tonight, shall I? Just to let you know how I'm settling in.'

'Well, perhaps not tonight, darling. I'm planning to stop off at the North Pole and see how Frostia's getting on. She's supposed to be having her pipes lagged, poor girl. And I want to keep my Ball clear in case there's news of Bacchus. But I'll flash you tomorrow, that's a promise. Hold on, here comes the next leap!'

It really wasn't an enjoyable ride. By the time we had endured two more hyper-leaps, me and my paper bag were well acquainted with each other. I'll spare you the details. Let's just say that I was more than relieved when the coach slowed to a mid-air halt.

'Here we are,' said Mother. 'Journey's end. For you, at any rate.'

24

Queasily, I looked through the window. Up here, the clouds had cleared and we could see the landscape spread beneath us far, far below. It wasn't much to look at. Mountains, mountains, nothing but mountains. On the top of the highest stood a turreted castle. Starkacre Hall, presumably. A local storm was currently raging about its tall towers. We were too far up to hear the thunder, but you could see the lightning flashes quite clearly. The storm was confined to the area around the castle. Everywhere else, it was a fine night.

'Oh dear,' sighed Mother. 'So ... unnecessarily over the top. Oh well. Each to her own. Hold tight, we're going down.'

And down we went, swooping through nothingness, while I clung to the strap with white knuckles and tried to come to some arrangement with my stomach.

There was a gentle bump as wheels and hoofs met with the cracked, wet flagstones of the courtyard. All around us, the storm was doing its worst. Thunder, lightning, high winds, buckets of rain, the full monty. Nice weather it wasn't.

There came a splashing sound and Muckbucket, with his jacket over his head, wrenched open the door. Freezing rain blew in on the back of a bitter wind.

'Shall I get the trunk down, ma'am?' he enquired.

'Yes please, Muckbucket. Take it up the steps, if you'd be so kind. And shut the door. We're getting rather wet in here.'

Muckbucket slammed the door shut. The coach wobbled as he climbed on to the running-board and wrestled the trunk down.

'So, Wilma,' said Mother briskly. 'This is goodbye.'

'Oh,' I said, surprised. 'Aren't you coming in?'

'No, darling. Not tonight. I'm behind already and I just can't spare the time. But do give my love to Auntie and tell her I'll visit soon. No, actually, tell her I'll write. Yes, I'll write. No, better still, I'll give her a flash on the Ball. We can catch up on all the news. Yes, I'll do that. Oh, before you go, I've got a little present for her.'

She reached into her reticule and withdrew a small enamel pot, labelled GOUT CREAM in her own neat, flowing hand. There was also a slim parcel wrapped in black paper and adorned with a black ribbon.

'What is it?'

'Gout cream. My special recipe, tell her.'

'No, I mean, what's in the parcel?'

'It's a lovely photograph of us all together, taken at the welcome-home party we threw for Maud. I've had it blown up and tastefully framed. We're all in it, the whole family.'

'Apart from Great-Aunt Angria,' I pointed out.

'Well – no.'

'Who wasn't invited.'

'Well – no.'

'Again.'

'Well – no. I *meant* to, but somehow ...' Her voice trailed away.

'This'll put her in a great mood, then, won't it?' I said, sticking the present into the capacious inner pocket of my cloak.

'Hmm. Perhaps it wasn't the best choice of gifts. Oh well.' Mother gave a little sigh. 'She's always complaining she never sees us. Now she can. Anyway, I'm sure she'll find the cream helps.'

More sploshy noises came from outside. A half-drowned Muckbucket, back from depositing the trunk. He yanked the door open and stood aside, waiting for me to climb down.

'There's noises comin' from that there trunk,' he remarked. 'Sounds like a c–'

Luckily, a peal of thunder drowned out the rest.

'Goodbye, Mother,' I cried heartily, shooting up out of the seat and planting a kiss on her pale cheek. 'See you in three days. Give my love to Daddy.'

'Goodbye, Wilma,' said Mother. 'Try and be as helpful as you can. Remember, underneath it all, she's only a poor old lady. Don't forget to clean your teeth. And *do* brush your hair.'

'I will,' I promised, with a merry little wave. And jumped out into the deluge and down into a puddle.

'Mother will miss you! Don't stand in the wet, darling, go in! You're getting soaked.'

'It's all right,' I bellowed, over the noise of the storm. 'I'll see you off.'

I *can* be charming when I feel like it.

Muckbucket slammed the door and trudged around to the front. Clint and Horace both tried to kick him as he went past, I noticed. Ah, the close bond that exists between horse and man.

Heavy rain lashed down as I watched him pick up the reins, willing him to hurry up. My charming smile was wearing thin, rather like my cloak, which has got too small for me and won't fasten properly at the neck, so the hood won't stay up. It felt like the sky giant was pouring a bucket of water down my back.

The courtyard was enclosed within high walls and there wasn't room to pick up speed by racing along the ground, so, quite simply, the two horses just rose vertically upwards with the Night Coach keeping level behind. It doesn't look as good as taking off at high speed with a thunder of hoofs, but it works. As soon as the whole caboodle cleared the walls, it zoomed off into the storm-tossed night. The last thing I caught a glimpse of was Mother's gloved hand raised in a queenly gesture of farewell.

I turned to face the castle. Lightning flared. Thunder cracked. The rain turned to hail, smashing down out of the sky and bouncing off the lid of my trunk which had been dumped at the top of the crumbling flight of stone steps leading to the great door.

This was it, then. I was on my own. A zillion miles from home in the middle of a thunderstorm in the courtyard of a strange castle with nothing to comfort me apart from a cuddly frog, a hot-water bottle, my guitar, a great many sweet things and a demented cat.

Oh well, I thought. Best foot forward. And I clutched my cloak about me and waded across the flagstones.

4. STARKACRE HALL

Two crumbly stone lions flanked the steps. Or maybe they were poodles. Hard to tell. The workmanship was very primitive. One was missing an ear and the other an eye, but that didn't stop them glaring as I approached. I couldn't be sure, what with the rain and the thunder and everything, but I thought one of them gave a low snarl as I passed between them.

'Get lost, rock head,' I muttered, less than impressed. Getting stone animals to snarl on demand is no big deal. I've been doing it myself since I was a toddler. Simple Animation Spell, nothing to it.

The lid of my trunk was rattling up and down, accompanied by wails of feline fury. Denzil had *really* had enough.

'Take it easy, Denzil,' I shouted, over the thunder. 'I'll let you out as soon as we're inside.'

Wind whipping my soaked cloak, battered by hail, I stood on the top step and stared up at the iron-studded oak door. How was I to get in? As far as I could see, there was no knocker. No handle, no knob, no bell-pull, no key, no lock, no Magicom, no letter box. Just door, door, and more door, soaring up into shadow.

Just then, a vivid flash of lightning illuminated the ghastly features of a hideously ugly gargoyle placed dead centre above the lintel. It had crossed eyes and a massive, grinning mouth. I made a face at it. Instantly, the eyes uncrossed and an enormous gout of freezing cold water came spurting out. It was the biggest spit that anyone has ever spat at me, including my sisters, who are a hard act to follow, I can tell you.

I leaped hastily to one side to avoid it, barking my shin on the trunk. Denzil yowled even louder. I stooped to rub my leg – luckily, as it happens, because a falling lump of masonry came hurtling down from aloft, travelling through the space where my head had just been and landing a centimetre from my foot.

And then – slowly, in absolute silence, with no hint of squealing hinges or ominous grinding – the door opened.

Inside – beyond – lay total blackness. And I mean *total*.

Ever had the feeling that someone was trying to put the willies up you?

It takes a *lot* to put the willies up me. I've got Frostia and Scarlettine for sisters.

'Right,' I said stoutly. 'Here we go, Denzil. This is where the fun begins.'

And I grabbed the handle of my trunk and dragged it into the castle.

I hovered just inside the threshold, unable to see a thing beyond the end of my nose. Behind me, silently and firmly, the door closed. The noise of the storm was instantly cut off, as though someone had reached out and turned off the volume. All there was now was the darkness and the silence.

Actually, the silence wasn't total. It had scuttling noises in it and the odd, echoing drip. The darkness was, however, very dark indeed.

I was prepared, though. I'd brought my own supply of Magic Candles, remember? No flies on Wilma. I crouched down and, working by feel only, unclipped the catch of my trunk and raised the lid.

I reeled back as a frantic ball of whirring claws shot out, scrabbled over my shoulder and took off into the dark, scratching my left ear in the process. There was the sound of panicky paws scrabbling across stone, then nothing.

'Denzil!' I shouted. My voice echoed spookily. 'You come back here, you stupid cat!'

(Except it sounded more like caaa … aaa … aaatt … t!)

Nothing.

Muttering, I stooped and fumbled around inside the trunk. Everything was covered in cat drool. Yuck. One of the packets of chocolate biscuits had been gnawed open and there were slimy crumbs everywhere, as well as bits of chewed stuffing from Graham and half a ton of cat hairs. I was beginning to think that bringing Denzil along for the ride hadn't been too good an idea.

I ate a couple of the biscuits anyway, for strength.

I finally located the bundle of Magic Candles, extracted one and held it out before me.

'Light!' I commanded. (Li … i … ight … t!)

Instantly, the wick flared with a slightly blue, steady flame. Magic Candles are infinitely superior to your average, common-or-garden candle. They are made of special Magic wax, which is self-adjusting and doesn't drip. They're terribly expensive, but well worth the money. (Well, not *my* money. I never buy them. I just pinch them from Peevish's pantry when his back's turned.)

Holding it up, I stared around.

I was standing in a large hall, decorated in a style that can only be described as Overblown Gothic. I mean, we have our share of ugly family heirlooms back home, plus the Ancestral Halls stretch into infinity, so we're not exactly fanatical about cleanliness. But this was ridiculous. Rotting tapestries sagged from the walls. The stone-flagged floors were thick with dust and mouse droppings. Horrible, big old pictures were hung around the place, so thickly draped with cobwebs that it was anybody's guess what lay beneath. I counted at least six decrepit suits of armour and enough rusty, wall-mounted weaponry to equip a fair-sized army, provided they didn't mind it all falling apart the minute they picked it up.

There was something else that caught my eye. Set on a raised dais slap in the centre of the room was a table draped with a black velvet cloth. Well, it was black once, before what looked like a hundred years' worth of dust had settled. Placed on top were two objects: an egg-timer in a black frame and a clock.

The egg-timer was the biggest one I had ever seen. If it had been put on the floor next to me, it would probably have come up to my armpit. The bottom bulb was getting very full. A fine stream of sand was slowly pouring from the top bulb, which only had a few centimetres of grains left.

The clock was an ugly, black marble affair. The hands pointed to eleven-thirty. I glanced at my wrist to check the accuracy, then remembered I didn't have a watch. (I'd lost my old one a week or so ago. I think it fell in the trifle when I was cooking.)

There was something else on the dais too. Next to the table was an old-fashioned spinning-wheel. It was heavily draped with cobwebs, but the shape was unmistakable. Funny thing to stick on prominent display in the centre of the hall. Oh well. Like Mother says, each to her own.

I wasn't sure where to try first. An imposing flight of winding steps led into the upper storeys. I wasn't sure, but I thought I heard a faint sound coming from just around the first bend. A sort of panting. Do mice pant?

'Hallooo … ooooo … ooo!' I called. 'Anybody up there … ere … ere … r?'

Nothing.

'Denzil … enzil … enzil … l!' I tried again. 'Where are you, you pest … est … est … t?'

Then I noticed the trail of paw prints outlined in the dust on the floor. They led across the hall and to one side of the staircase, passing under a vaulted arch and into a long stone passageway.

Crossly, I set off in pursuit. My coach sickness had worn off and I was more than ready for some proper food – or, at the very least, a cup of hot chocolate and maybe a crumpet or six. Where was everybody? Why was nobody here to welcome me, ask me about my journey, take my wet cloak and run me a nice hot bath before leading me to a loaded supper tray placed before a blazing fire? Was this a test of courage or something? If so, I could do without it.

The passageway was cold, damp and lined with yet more suits of armour in varying degrees of dilapidation. I carefully checked the shadows behind the legs, but there was no sign of Denzil. Plenty of spiders, though. At one point, something black leaped out and scurried across my foot, but it was only a rat. The floor was wet and slimy with mould, so I didn't have paw prints to follow.

Every so often, I came across doors set in the walls – ancient, secret-looking doors with dull brass knobs on. I tried them, but they all seemed to be locked. Every now and then, a pocket of freezing air took my breath away. Strange little gusts of wind puffed up my skirt. I thought I heard the heavy breathing sound again, coming from behind me, but when I turned, there was nothing there.

I couldn't shake off the feeling that someone – or some *thing* – was watching me.

'Denzil … enzil … enzil … l!' I called again, keeping my voice sweet though I could cheerfully have murdered him. 'Wilma's got a biscuit … iscuit … iscuit … t! Nice biscuit, all for you … ooo … ooo …'

I broke off. There was a noise coming from somewhere up ahead. It was the full-throated sound of an organ! I could feel the vibrations caused by the low notes coming up from the floor and into my boots.

Aha! At last, a sign of life. Perhaps supper wasn't too far off after all. Nobody had mentioned that Great-Aunt Angria was of a musical bent. She must be filling in time before I arrived, having a little fiddle on the organ. Not that the music was very lively. On the contrary, it was a gloomy dirge of deep, minor chords with loads of wrong notes added for good measure. 'Chopsticks' it wasn't.

I hurried along the passageway towards the thunderous sounds, which gradually swelled in volume to unpleasant, teeth-rattling levels. I passed beneath another arch. The passage now widened out into a chamber, which contained three more doors – taller, more imposing, with oak panels and bigger knobs. The appalling recital was coming from behind the one on the left. I could see it rattling.

I grasped hold of the knob. Rather to my surprise, considering all the door trouble I'd been having lately, it turned. The door swung open and I was hit in the face by a wall of sound.

Yes, there was an organ all right. And what an organ! It was a mighty construction of ornate, black ebony fretwork, vast pipes, stops, pedals, keyboards and cobwebs. It towered against the far wall, dominating the room, which was empty apart from a solitary music stand containing a single, yellow, dust-covered sheet of music.

Clashing, doom-laden chords thundered from the pipes as the keys moved up and down.

All by themselves.

Yes, you heard. There was nobody playing them. Honestly! After all that tramping about. Was I never to get any food?

'Oh, for crying out loud!' I snapped and stamped my foot. Instantly, the organ keys stopped moving and the final, ear-splitting chord wheezed into silence.

Then, very slowly, the organ stool swivelled in a half-circle. From the space just above came a dry, knowing chuckle. Seconds later, a pocket of icy air swept past me. The sheet music, caught in the back-draught, fluttered to the floor and blew about a bit, ending up wrapped around my foot. In kicking myself free, I caught sight of the title, written in faded, spidery writing: 'Fonata For Fcary Background Chordf'.

Well, what did you expect? The Birdie Song?

The chuckle came again, this time from behind me. The ghost, or invisible presence or whatever it called itself, was hanging in the doorway, intent on getting the last laugh. It was beginning to get on my nerves.

'Oh, shut up!' I snarled. 'Think you can play? Well, you can't, you're lousy.'

If cold air can bristle, that's what it did. I sensed a wave of icy fury directed at me, then it was gone.

'Good riddance!' I shouted. 'Try practising a few scales! Your left hand's all jerky!'

There's nothing that annoys me more than a pushy ghost. We have ghosts back in the Ancestral Halls, but we make it a policy to ignore them. They've long given up trying to get attention and just skulk quietly in corners, occasionally rattling the odd chain in a sullen sort of way. Well, you've got to be firm, or they try to take over.

I turned on my heel and stomped out of the organ room. What with Mother's lullaby and 'Fonata For Fcary

Background Chordf', I'd had quite enough doomy music for one day.

The door slammed shut behind me, rather abruptly, I thought.

I eyed the other two doors. I might as well take a look, seeing I was there. For some reason, I walked past the middle door and along to the one on the right. I tried the knob. This one turned too. I opened it a crack and poked my head around.

It wasn't a room at all, despite the posh door. It was a large, walk-in cupboard, full of brooms, buckets and various cleaning materials which, from the amount of cobwebs and spider activity, clearly hadn't been used in centuries. There was also a full-size skeleton propped in one corner.

Honestly. A skeleton in the cupboard. Talk about corny. It wasn't even a real one. I knew that because it had *Made in Way Hay* stamped on the skull and the feet had been put on backwards. We've got one just like it at home. We call it Fatty. Disgusted, I shut the door.

Then I walked back to the middle door. I wasn't quite sure why I had left it till last. There was something about it I didn't like. Just a feeling.

Still. I was here now.

I reached out and turned the knob.

5. RALPH

The first thing I noticed was the cold. Not your average freezing cold, like Frostia's palace, which is made entirely of ice. (Or *was*, until it all fell down around her ears, ha ha.) This was a different sort of cold. Clammy. Oppressive. The air shimmered and had a greasy feel which I recognized. A Magical force field had been set up. Looking round in the bluish light cast by my Candle, I knew why.

At first sight, it seemed as though the room was full of waxworks. They were dotted here and there, with no sense of order.

There was a shepherdess in a straw bonnet and printed muslin skirt. In one hand she held a crook. Nestling at her knee was a surprised-looking sheep.

There was a farmer, wearing a battered hat, a grubby smock and muddy boots. He had a pitchfork over his shoulder and straw in his beard, just in case there might be any doubt about his farming credentials.

There was a small boy in ragged jerkin and breeches, frozen in the act of making a rude face. His nose was wrinkled up and his tongue stuck out. There was a rascally gleam in his eye.

There was a tall, thin man in a three-cornered hat and dark frock coat holding a clipboard. He had *insurance* written all over him. (Well, not literally. That'd be daft.)

I stared around, my eyes falling on a milkmaid holding a jug of milk, a mild-looking little man in hiking boots with a map in his hand, a burly woodcutter with an axe and a fat little woman in a mob cap, her apron pocket full of pegs. There was a baker's boy with a tray of buns slung around his neck. There was a tiny, thumb-sucking girl holding a rag doll. There was a smooth-looking chap who I guessed was a salesman because he had *Magic Screens Inc.* stencilled on his briefcase. There was a wandering minstrel in a feathered hat, his fingers frozen on the strings of a mandolin. His mouth was open, as if he was just about to burst into song.

There were other animals as well as the sheep. A scruffy-looking mongrel dog with a defiant expression and a bone clamped in his teeth. A pig with a curly tail. A goat, with what looked like a half-eaten black woolly cardigan hanging from its mouth. There were cats too – three poor, scraggy old moggies, one black, one ginger, one with a single eye.

I was glad Denzil wasn't here to see this.

I walked up to the shepherdess and looked her in the eyes. She stared ahead. Not a flicker. I reached out a cautious finger to give her nose a tweak. Just before my finger touched, there was a faint crackling noise. I felt an unpleasant tingling in the tip, and my finger met with some sort of invisible barrier.

I withdrew it hastily. You don't mess with Magical force fields. Even the spiders knew that. It was the only place I'd come across so far that was cobweb-free.

You'll have gathered by now that what we had here wasn't a room full of waxworks. What we had here was a room full of real, live people. But enchanted people. People in the grip of a very, very strong spell.

Now, as you know, I am not easily spooked. I am, after all, the direct descendant of a proud line of wicked queens who dabble in witchcraft on a regular basis. I have a laboratory back home and have been known to conjure up a few nasty spells of my own when the mood takes me.

But this room gave me the creeps. The coldness. The greasy taste of the air. The unnatural stillness. All those sightless eyes, staring straight ahead. How long had they been like this? And what had they done to deserve such a fate?

'You're not shuposhed to be in here.'

The voice came from behind me. Stifling a cry, I whirled around, almost setting fire to my sleeve with the Candle.

Standing on all fours in the doorway was a large grey timber wolf! It had eyes like yellow coins. A long red tongue curled like a ribbon from its mouth, which contained more teeth than I cared to count. It was slavering a bit.

'Sheesh!' I gasped. 'Don't do that! Where did you spring from? I didn't hear you come in. What quiet paws you have!'

'All the better to shtalk you with,' replied the wolf immediately, then sat back on its haunches, looking rather pleased with itself.

Stalking me, eh? Well, that solved the mystery of the heavy breathing at any rate.

We stared at each other. From somewhere in the castle, a distant clock began to chime midnight. How time flies when you're enjoying yourself.

'Go on, then,' growled the wolf. It sounded eager. 'Shay the necsht bit.'

'What next bit?'

'*You* know.'

Now, personally, I'm not keen on talking animals. I think animals should be animals, no more, no less. Once, when we were younger, Scarlettine used a Speech Spell on Gavin, her pet pony, but all he ever talked about was hay, hay, more hay and the discomfort of having to hold interesting conversations about hay with a bit in his mouth. Everyone agreed he was a pain in the neck and after he complained for the millionth time about her weight, Scarlettine removed the spell and Gavin went back to blissful silence.

'No,' I said coldly. 'I don't know.'

'*You* know,' said the wolf again. It was quivering a bit. Its claws were flexing in and out with excitement. 'About how big my earsh are. Shay it.'

41

'*No.*'

'Why not?'

'Because. I don't even know you. Why should I pay you compliments? Anyway, they're not particularly big. Just normal-sized, really.'

The wolf's furry face wrinkled in disappointment. There was a long pause while it ran its long red tongue over its teeth. Then it said meaningfully:

'I ecshpect you *really* like picking flowersh.'

Picking flowers? What madness was this?

'Look,' I said. 'I don't know who you are, but ...'

'*Rrralph!*' barked the wolf, from deep in its throat.

'What?'

'That'sh my name. Ralph.'

'Well, Ralph,' I said crisply, 'this might come as news to you, but I'm an invited guest. My name is —'

'I know who you are,' he interrupted. 'You're Her great-neesh. Wilma.'

'*Princess* Wilma to you. And seeing you've already admitted to stalking me, you're well aware that I've spent the last half hour stomping around this castle looking for my cat who seems to have gone to ground along with everyone else. I'm cold, wet and hungry and quite frankly, I'd like a bit of service around here.'

'You might *like* it,' said Ralph, with a sneer. 'But you won't *get* it. No shervantsh here. Mishtresh don't hold with 'em.'

That figured. All those cobwebs everywhere, it stood to reason that home help didn't feature in the great scheme of things at Starkacre Hall.

'By Mistress, I take it you're referring to my Great-

Aunt Angria?' I enquired.

'Yesh. The Thirteenth Faerie,' said Ralph, in tones of deepest respect. You could hear the capital letters.

'And do you happen to know where she is? Or do I spend the rest of the night playing Hunt the Auntie?'

'I'll take you to Her,' said Ralph. He spoke rather stiffly. I don't think he was taking to *me* much. 'Like I shaid, you shouldn't be in here anyway. The Room of Living Shtatuesh ish barred to all but Mishtresh.'

'Then I suggest she fits a padlock,' I said sharply.

'Well, I might just advishe Her to do that,' retorted Ralph, through gritted teeth.

'Good!' I snapped. 'Lead on.'

'I will.'

'Thank you.'

'Don't mention it.'

Our icy little exchange ground to a halt. He glared, folded away his tongue, rose to his feet and padded from the room without a backward glance. I followed behind, glad to leave the place. The door closed behind us, leaving the silent ranks of enchanted ones once again on their own in the cold dark.

Outside, Ralph picked up speed and trotted back along the passageway at a fair old lope. I needed all my breath to keep up. That was OK by me. At least we didn't have to talk.

I kept my eyes open, but there was still no sign of Denzil.

We reached the main hall. Ralph slowed to allow me to catch up.

'Up the shtairsh,' he said shortly. 'After you.'

'No, no,' I said. 'After *you*.' Well, he was a bit odd. You can't be too careful.

'Ladiesh firsht,' insisted Ralph.

'But you know the way,' I said obstinately. It was stalemate. We stood there, glowering at each other.

'Shide by shide, perhapsh?' suggested Ralph.

It seemed a reasonable compromise. I gave a short nod and set off up the flight of wide, curving steps. Ralph padded alongside, giving me sly sideways looks that Grandma always refers to as 'old-fashioned'.

The stairs seemed to go on forever. Round and round they spiralled. After a few minutes I was sweating and scarlet and had to pause for a rest.

'You're not very fit, are you?' remarked Ralph, with a lupine sneer. 'I can shee you're not ushed to ecshershishe.'

'At least I can *say* it,' I snapped. Honestly. Talk about personal.

'What'sh that shuposhed to mean?'

'Well, let's face it. You have trouble getting the old jaws around S, don't you? You can't say it properly.'

'Yesh I can.'

'No you can't. It sounds like you've got a mouthful of shrimps. Anyway, I get plenty of exercise. I don't need to run mindlessly around all night in a pack baying at the moon, if that's what you're suggesting.'

'You should try walking in the woodsh. That'sh fine ecshershishe, walking in the woodsh.' He eyed me up and down, adding: 'You're very pink. Why don't you take your cloak off?'

'I'm fine,' I said shortly. I don't take fashion tips from wolves.

'It'sh a very *warm*-looking cloak. Lined, ish it? Nishe, fleeshy lining to keep the wind out?'

'No, actually,' I said, staring at him. What was all this about?

'Unushual shade for a cloak. Brown. Have you ever thought about another colour? *Red*, for ecshample?'

He was pretending to be casual, but there was a very strange glint in his eye. I decided to give him a wide berth as soon as we reached the top of this confounded staircase.

'No,' I snapped. 'I've never been fond of red. One of my sisters wears it all the time. Not that it's any of your business. Now, can we get on?'

'Shuit yourshelf,' said Ralph, quite huffy now.

We climbed the rest of the stairs in silence. There weren't many more, but even so I was feeling quite light-headed when we finally reached the top. I stood, swaying and holding on to the banister, trying not to gasp too much. The remark about my lack of fitness had got to me.

When I recovered, I held up my Magic Candle and stared around. Before us was yet another passageway with yet more flipping doors. This passageway differed in that it had wood panelling and for once there were no suits of armour. What it *did* have was dribbly candles set in niches. They were the cheap, ordinary kind, but they cast a reasonable enough glow. I blew out my Candle. They don't last for ever. It doesn't do to waste them.

'How much further?' I enquired. I'd really had enough of all this.

'No further. We're here,' said Ralph. And he loped up

to the first door, raised a paw and scratched at the flaking, dark green paint.

There was a short pause – then it opened, all by itself. Self-opening doors seemed to be a feature of Starkacre Hall.

Ralph padded in.

And me? I followed.

6. GREAT-AUNT ANGRIA

The first thing I noticed was the smell. It was a sickly combination of smoke, mothballs and the sharp tang of liniment. I stood in the doorway trying not to sneeze, my eyes drawn to the large four-poster bed that took up the best part of one wall. It had carved feet, like a dragon's. The curtains hanging from the rail were little more than rags. The rumpled bedding looked as though it could do with a change. (But then again, so can mine.)

Next to the bed was a cluttered side table containing millions of pots of pills, jars of ointment and sinister little black bottles of patent medicine.

There was a fire burning in the hearth. The flames leaped and danced, sending shadows scuttling into corners. Every so often, a puff of black smoke billowed

47

into the room. The chimney needed sweeping, that was for sure.

Facing the fire was a big, old, high-backed armchair. A walking stick with a carved silver knob was propped against one arm.

Ralph had already commandeered the threadbare rug that lay before the hearth. He lay doggy-like on his back with all four legs stuck stupidly in the air, hogging the heat, having a good old back scratch, generally making himself at home.

'So ye've arrived,' said a cracked, ancient voice from the chair. 'Come over here, girl. Let's have a look at ye.'

Here goes, then, I thought. And I walked to the chair, rounded it ... *and came face to face with Grandma*!

Of course, it wasn't Grandma. It was Great-Aunt Angria. But what a shock! You'd think someone might have mentioned that they were identical twins. They both had the same tiny, shrunken frame, the same beaky nose and the same hooded green eyes with the same bags underneath. They even dressed alike, in crow-black robes topped with an assortment of woolly cardigans, raggy old scarves and shabby shawls.

The one thing that set them apart was the hair. Grandma goes in for neat, corrugated curls, tidily tucked away beneath a hairnet. In contrast, Great-Aunt Angria's hair was like something that had crawled out of a swamp. There was masses of the stuff – matted, grey, tangled swathes of it, sprouting wildly out of her head and coiling down into her lap.

Well, at least we had horrible hair in common.

Her feet were in a much worse condition than

Grandma's too. They were encased in a pair of thick woolly socks, and propped up on a low footstool. They looked swollen. Definitely puffy round the ankles.

But, hey! Where were my manners? I gave a formal little curtsy.

'How do you do, Great-Aunt Angria?' I said, stepping forward with my hand held out. My boot just touched the side of the footstool. Just brushed against it, that's all.

'Me feet!' screamed my auntie, in sudden terror. 'Don't go near me feet!'

'Sorry,' I said hastily, stepping back.

'I should bloomin' well think so. Clumsy girl!'

'Still got problems, then?' I enquired.

'O' course I got problems!' shouted Great-Aunt Angria. 'Had blasted problems all me life. Corns, chilblains, hard skin, fallen arches, hammer toes, verrucas, bunions, ingrowin' nails, athlete's foot, houseboy's heel, badminton ankle, I've had 'em all.'

'Houseboy's heel? I've never heard of that,' I remarked politely.

'Same as housemaid's knee, but in the heel.'

'And badminton ankle would be … ?'

'Like tennis elbow, but …'

' … in the foot.' I nodded. 'Right. My word, you really have suffered, haven't you?'

'Sufferin's not the word, girl. And now, to crown it all, I've gone an' got the blasted gout! Haven't been able to get me blasted shoes on for a blasted fortnight!'

'Ah,' I said. 'I might be able to help you there. Mother sent this.'

I reached into my pocket, withdrew the small jar and presented it with a flourish.

'What's this?' mumbled Great-Aunt Angria, snatching it away and peering suspiciously at the label.

'Gout Cream. Mother's own recipe. It never fails, apparently.'

'Aye, well they all say that. We'll see.' Ungraciously, she stuffed the jar down the side of the armchair. 'Now. Stand back a bit. I wants to have a look at ye.'

I stood back and tried not to fidget under her hard green gaze.

'So,' she said, after a good full minute of rude staring. 'Ye're Veronica's youngest. Not much of a looker. Name?'

'Wilma,' I said, rather stiffly. I was aware that I wasn't about to win any beauty contests, what with my shabby old cloak, soggy boots and horrible hair, which had gone even more bonkers than usual as a result of the rain. But still. Who was she to talk?

'Well, young Wilma. What do ye make of Starkacre Hall so far, eh? What did ye think of my storm?'

'Very nice,' I said politely. 'Very – er – theatrical.'

'Aye. I does a good storm, me. Enjoy the organ recital?' She looked at me sideways and gave a short cackle. It was clear that she rather hoped I had found it unsettling.

'Not much,' I said, with a shrug. 'I'm not a great fan of phantom organists. And there were an awful lot of wrong notes.'

Great-Aunt Angria gave a sniff.

'Aye. Well, maybe the ghosts at Starkacre don't quite meet the high standards of the Ancestral Halls, but they do me. See anything else of interest? I know ye've had a good old snoop around. Quite the little Nosy Parker, ain't ye? Been watching ye in the Glass.'

For the first time, I noticed a small, silver-backed mirror in her wrinkled hand. It was an old-fashioned Scrying Glass. You don't see them around much these days. Crystal Ball technology has long since taken over.

'She was poking around in The Room of Living Shtatuesh, Mishtresh,' chipped in Ralph, a born taleteller if ever there was one. He sneered at me and scratched triumphantly at a flea.

'So I saw.'

'I did tell her it wash private,' he added pompously.

'It should have been locked, then,' I shot back, adding: 'And I wasn't being nosy. I was looking for my cat.'

'Saw that too.' Great-Aunt Angria scowled. 'What in tarnation made ye bring a blasted cat here? Can't stand the blasted things. Any cat comes round here, I zaps 'em an' sticks 'em in with all the other blighters what's crossed me over the years.'

'I noticed,' I said, thinking of the trio of poor, bedraggled old moggies I'd seen earlier. 'You'd better not do that to Denzil. Mrs Pudding would go mad.'

'Mrs Who?'

'Mrs Pudding, our cook. Denzil belongs to her. He's on loan. Sort of.'

'Well, just keep 'im away from me is all I'm sayin'.'

'I will,' I promised. 'When I find him.'

'So ye've got a Mrs Puddin' now,' reflected Great-Aunt Angria. 'After my time. There was a proper chef there in my day. Basin, that was his name. Chef Basin.

Came from foreign parts. Shouted a lot. Daft little moustache. Did a lovely soufflé, though. I wonder what 'appened to 'im?'

'Who knows?' I said. 'Anyway, it's Mrs Pudding now. Hey!' A thought struck me. 'Shame the two families didn't intermarry. Ha, ha, ha. They'd be known as the Pudding-Basins.'

Well, I thought it was quite good, but nobody else laughed.

'I s'pose 'tis all different now, back there. My, my. How time passes.' Great-Aunt Angria stared into the flames for a moment. Then she looked up and snapped:

'How come yer ma didn't drop in to see me? Must be over a coupla hundred years since I seen her. Or any of 'em, come to that.'

'She's doing the Round,' I hastened to explain. 'She's ever so busy. Never a minute. You know what it's like, being Queen of the Night.'

'Nope,' said Great-Aunt Angria, with more than a touch of bitterness. 'Can't say I do. As ye might expect, *that* job went to Grimelza.'

It was the first time I'd ever heard Grandma referred to by her name. Mother and Aunt Maud call her Mama. To the rest of the family, she's always Grandma. Everyone else calls her Ma'am.

'Anyway,' I went on quickly, 'anyway, Mother sends her love and says she'll flash you on your Crystal Ball.'

'Ain't got a Crystal Ball. Me old one wore out years ago. Never got round to replacin' it.'

'Oh, but you should. The new ones are *ever* so good.'

'Don't care for newfangled things. Too many blasted

newfangled things these days. Anyway, I got no call for one,' growled my auntie. 'No one I wants to talk to. I got me Scryin' Glass. That does me.'

'She sent something else.' I reached into my pocket and withdrew the slim, black, beribboned parcel that Mother had given me.

'What is it? Chocolates or summint?' There was a flicker of interest in her eyes.

'It's a photograph. It's got all of us in. The whole family. We had it taken at Aunt Maud's welcome-home party.'

Oops. Perhaps I shouldn't have mentioned that.

'Oh, is that all?' She scowled. 'Thought it might be chocolates. Well, take the blinkin' paper off, then. I can't be havin' with all that tarradiddle at my age. Ralph! Leave yer blasted fleas in peace for two minutes and fetch my specs. Over on the table somewhere.'

'Conshider it done, Mishtresh.' Instantly, Ralph was on his feet, all brisk efficiency. He padded off, tail waving importantly, while I fought with the wrapping paper.

'Done it?' said Great-Aunt Angria impatiently. 'Come on, come on, pass it over. *And stay away from me feet!*'

I placed the photograph in her lap and moved behind her chair, well away from the swollen extremities displayed on the footstool. Ralph came trotting back, a pair of dusty-looking glasses dangling from his jaws. He dropped them gently into her hand. He placed his chin on her knee and gazed lovingly into her face, obviously hoping for a kind word or a pat. It was quite sickening.

'Get back over there, Ralph!' cried Great-Aunt Angria. 'Can't ye do nothin' right? Ye've got 'em all slimy!'

She pointed to the rug. The wolf cringed at the harsh

words, then slunk back to the fireplace and began to lick a paw in a dejected sort of way. Great-Aunt Angria rubbed her spectacles with the sleeve of her cardigan, then set them on her nose. She raised the photograph close to her eyes and peered.

'So who are all these, then? Do I know 'em all?'

'Well, of course, there's me. There, see? In the blue dress. They've cut my head off, but you probably recognize me anyway.'

'I do. I recognizes yer fat stomach.' Fighting words, which I chose to ignore.

'And then there's Grandma,' I said, leaning over her shoulder and pointing to the centre of the group, where Grandma sat in pride of place, hands folded over her stick.

'Hmm,' said my auntie, studying her twin. 'Age ain't done her no favours, that's for sure. When did she cut 'er hair off? What's with the hairnet? Is that supposed to be a smile on her face? What's she so flippin' pleased about?'

'She's happy because Maud's finally come home,' I explained. 'Remember Maud? Mother's sister? She went missing for some years. Didn't want to be Queen of the Night when Grandma retired, so she ran away to join the gypsies and married a Parsley, so Mother took the job on. That's her, look, with the daisy chain and the guitar.'

'Hmph. Looks like one o' them hippies. Who's this next to her?'

'That's her husband, New Uncle Frank. He doesn't say much. Well, anything, actually. And see that boy there? The one holding the dog with the shiny jacket and blue shoes and greasy hair?'

54

'I don't see no dog with a shiny jacket.'

'No, no, the boy's got the jacket. He's Alvis, their son. He's a bit weird, but all right, actually. And that's Mother, but you can't see her too well because of her Aura. And there's Daddy and Uncle Bacchus. The snooty one in white is Frostia.'

'My lordy, how she's grown. Queen of the Snow now, right? And yer other sister's Queen of Mirrors, so I hear.'

'Right. Scarlettine. The show-off in red, blowing kisses to the camera. See?'

'Hmm. Got time to put on all that lipstick, you'd think she'd find a moment to write and thank me for that postal order I sent.'

'She wouldn't,' I said, never one to miss an opportunity to bad-mouth Scarlettine. 'She is *soooo* selfish.'

'And this was taken at the welcome-'ome party, ye say?'

'Yep.'

'Funnily enough, I don't recall ever receivin' an invite.'

Oooer. Dangerous waters ahead.

'Well, it wasn't exactly a *party*,' I amended. 'More of an informal get-together. Slice of cake, couple of balloons. Nothing *major* ...'

'Ah, shut yer lyin' trap!' screamed Great-Aunt Angria, so loudly and suddenly that I jumped. Well, actually, it wasn't so much the shout that did it. It was her hair. I've heard of a bad hair day – well, every day is a bad hair day for me – but this was ridiculous.

My auntie's hair seemed to have acquired a life of its own. It began to wriggle and lash about. It was as though

55

she had a lap full of snakes. Great, long grey strands lifted from her shoulders and flew about, whipping the air in defiance of gravity. It really was quite unsettling. I moved away, out of range. Ralph gave a little whimper and looked anxious.

'Whoa!' I said. 'Now, now! Calm down.'

'I said *shut up*! Ye're as bad as the rest of 'em. Excuses, excuses, always blasted excuses!' She slammed the photograph face down on the floor. I distinctly heard the glass crack.

A short silence fell after this outburst. The hair was still writhing about all over the place, as though in the grip of its own miniature gale. Her face was twisted and her mouth worked furiously. I've never seen anyone so angry.

Actually, that was a good name for her. From then on, I privately thought of her as Aunt Angry. I didn't say it to her face, mind.

'Look,' I ventured after a bit. 'It was an oversight. Nobody meant to …'

'Didn't ye hear me? I don't want to hear no more about it. I turned my back on the lot of 'em years ago, and as far as I'm concerned, 'tis stayin' turned. Anyway, there's work to be done. No doubt ye'll be wantin' to know why ye're here.'

'Yes,' I said, relieved at the change of subject. Her hair was settling down now, I noticed. She must be getting over her paddy. 'I do. I must admit I'm curious. You can tell me all about it. Over a spot of supper perhaps?'

'Ye can eat afterwards. 'Tis easiest to show ye. Get my stick.'

I reached around the chair, picked up the stick – and

almost dropped it as a surge of Magical current zoomed up my arm. Ah. It was one of *those* Sticks. Grandma has one just like it. I should have guessed from the little lightning bolt carved into the silver knob at the top. Only the very best sorceresses have Sticks like this. They're handed down from mother to daughter. (Well, they should be. Grandma hasn't shown any signs of letting go of hers yet.)

'Don't touch the knob, fool girl! Didn't they teach ye nothin'? Hold it lower down, away from the Power source. Now then. Draw a Ring round my chair. Make it big enough to stand in. And *mind my blasted feet*!'

Keeping my fingers well away from the knob, I did as she instructed. The tip of the Stick left a pale green glow on the floorboards as I drew the circle. It wobbled a bit, because I was nervous. Ralph slunk over and sat next to the footstool.

'Right,' I said. 'Done. Now what?'

'Now we go down,' said Aunt Angry. And she raised one gnarled finger.

There was a loud bang, a white flash, a puff of green smoke – and down we went.

7. THE DUNGEON LABORATORY

It all happened incredibly quickly. One second I was in Great-Aunt Angria's room, and the next, I found myself in the dungeons of Starkacre Hall, watching green smoke disperse and holding on to my tummy, which continued on down even though the rest of me had stopped.

'Can't take the pace, eh? Made yer knees wobble?' sneered Aunt Angry. She was still ensconced in her armchair, which had also been transported, along with the footstool and Ralph, who suddenly rose, left the Ring and made off into the shadows.

'Not at all,' I lied, straightening up. 'It was a bit sudden. Took me by surprise.'

'Aye. Well, it saves all the steps. Can't be havin' with stairs these days. Not with me feet.'

I looked around. A solitary Magic Candle set in a niche in the wall sensed our presence and began to glow. It had obviously been used a lot and was nearing the end of its life, but it still cast a reasonable light.

Now, castle dungeons are much of a muchness. Chilly, dank, drippy caverns linked by a series of narrow passageways with small, barred cells set into the walls. A dungeon is, of course, an excellent place to set up a laboratory. Things occasionally go wrong with Magical experiments. It's easy to accidentally set fire to the curtains or frighten the servants rigid. If you're going to mess with Magic, you need somewhere private and preferably uncluttered. I myself have a lab in the dungeons of the Ancestral Halls. Although I am not naturally tidy, I pride myself on the fact that it's all very orderly. My work bench is always clear, apart from my Bunsen burner, test tubes and microscope. I keep my various Magical herbs and potions in alphabetical order and always make sure that any equipment I use goes back in its proper place.

Aunt Angry had also chosen to set up a lab in the dungeon. Well, *set up* isn't quite the phrase I'm looking for. *Fling in* would be more appropriate. Quite frankly, I have never seen a bigger shambles in all my life.

There were slithering piles of ancient books, all brown and mouldy with damp; dozens of splitting cardboard boxes spilling their miscellaneous contents all over the floor; bags full of fossils; baskets full of dried toadstools; sagging shelves containing hundreds of dusty bottles with the tops left off; a telescope; an accordion; one enormous boot with a small tree growing out of it; bundles of old

Wands tied up with string; a rusty cauldron full of bent nails; a mangle; the obligatory stuffed crocodile hanging crookedly from a hat stand; a set of golf clubs; a clutch of worn-out broomsticks – well, I could go on all night. Everything was just dumped any old where with no system whatsoever. Utter chaos.

'It could do with a sort-out, I s'pose,' said Aunt Angry, with a sniff. 'I ain't got round to it, with me feet.'

'Have a fire, did you?' I enquired, staring at the blackened work bench, which was mostly burned away. The remaining bit was all charred and covered in soot.

'Left the Bunsen burner on overnight. Blasted draught must have caught it.'

'Perhaps you ought to get someone in,' I suggested. 'It could do with a little light dusting, don't you think?' Several skips and a blooming great bonfire was what it could do with, but I was trying to be tactful.

'Nah,' said my auntie, shaking her head. 'I don't 'old with servants. Can't trust 'em. I'm all right on me own. I got Ralph and me Power. I don't need nobody.'

Suddenly, from somewhere over in a far, shadowy corner, there came the sound of lapping. Water was being scooped up by a long tongue and thrown down a throat.

'Ralph!' shrieked Aunt Angry. 'Are ye drinkin' from that Magic Pool again? What 'ave I told ye?'

There was a short pause, then Ralph came slinking back. He had a guilty expression and his jaws were dripping. His tail was between his legs.

'Shorry, Mishtresh,' he mumbled. 'Don't know what came over me.'

'I do, then,' said my auntie sternly. ''Tis that old instinct thing again, ain't it? The call o' the wild. See a hand, got to bite it. See a moon, got to howl at it. See a rabbit, got to chase it. See a pool o' water, got to drink from it. See a mob cap and a pair o' specs, can't keep yer blasted paws off. Ye got to *fight* it, Ralph. Ye're domesticated now.'

'I know,' said Ralph, hanging his head, obviously highly embarrassed.

Good. He needed taking down a peg or two.

What was that about the mob cap and the specs?

'Anyway,' said my auntie. 'This won't get the baby bathed. Pass me Stick.'

I looked down and, rather to my surprise, found I was still holding it.

'Why?' I said nervously. 'What are you going to do with it?'

'What d'ye think? 'Tis a walkin' Stick. I'm gonna walk with it. Try as I will I can't never get this blasted chair to set down just where I wants it. Come on, come on, hand it over.'

I passed her the Stick. There followed a whole lot of moaning and cries of woe as she put her poor old feet to the floor and struggled upright. I thought again how tiny she was, just like Grandma. She took a step forward. I went to help.

'Get off,' she snapped, smacking at my hand. 'I don't need no help. I can do it meself, once I gets me balance.'

I noticed, though, that she put a hand on Ralph's back for support as we slowly made our way to the far corner in which lay the Magic Pool.

I'm not familiar with Magic Pools. Like Scrying Glasses, they've gone out of fashion. Besides, they're associated with Fairies, who everyone knows are wimps. As I've already mentioned, these days, if you want to know what's happening in the wonderful world of Myth and Magic, you use a Crystal Ball. They're faster, more reliable and you can carry the smaller models in your pocket.

But I must admit that I was quite impressed. Magic Pools are traditionally found in sun-dappled woodland glades, surrounded by ferns, flowers and picturesque toadstools. This one, however, was set in a dark corner of a grotty dungeon and would have looked silly with all that frippery. There were no extras. It was just a plain, circular pool of dark, still water, probably a couple of metres across. It was sunk into the floor and edged with good-quality tiles of black marble. It looked functional. I approved.

'What does it show?' I asked, taking a professional interest. 'Past, present and future?'

'Yep. 'Tis a good one, this is. Ye gets what ye pays for. Came with a four-hundred-year guarantee. Had it overhauled recently. Too many dead spiders floatin' about, interfered with the reception. Supposed to keep it clean.' She glared at Ralph, who lay down and put his paws over his head, awash with shame.

'What are we going to watch?' I asked.

'Ah.' For the first time since my arrival, Great-Aunt Angry smiled. It wasn't a particularly pleasant smile. 'Well now, girl, I'll tell ye. We're goin' to watch a certain event that 'appened a long time before ye was born. Make yerself useful. Drag over a coupla them orange crates over there. This is gonna take a bit o' time. Got to get the weight off me pins.'

I collected the orange crates and set them side by side at the edge of the Pool.

'There's a cushion over there, by the broomsticks.'

I went back and collected it. By now, my stomach was beginning to grumble. Fascinating though all this was, I hoped it wasn't going to take too long.

'Whooo!' said my auntie, sinking down with a sigh of relief. 'That's better. Now then. Watch carefully. Ye might learn somethin'.'

She took her Stick, held it out over the Pool and moved it slowly across the surface in a great, sweeping arc. As she did so, she closed her eyes and muttered under her breath. The dark surface rippled as the shadow of the Stick moved across it. Suddenly, it began to boil, giving off clouds of purplish steam.

Then it cleared — and I found myself looking into another time, another place, another world.

8. THE MAGIC POOL

The scene was set in a palatial hall. Crystal chandeliers, marble pillars, velvet drapes, lots of gold leaf – you know the sort of thing. A small orchestra was playing soundlessly on a balcony. Footmen in red livery glided around quietly with drinks and nibbles. Men in white wigs and braided frock coats stood mouthing silently to glittering ladies in brightly coloured crinolines, who mouthed back to them.

'Hang on,' said Great-Aunt Angry. 'Volume needs adjustin'.'

She fumbled with the silver knob on her Stick. Instantly, there was a loud babble of voices and the sound of merry violins. Honestly, it was so real that I felt I could reach out and grab a sausage roll from a passing tray.

A long, red-carpeted aisle led to the far end of the hall. There, raised high on a dais, sat a king and queen on two golden thrones. You could tell they were royalty because they wore crowns and smug expressions. Between them was a cradle, vastly overdecorated with pink ribbons and frothy white lace. Every so often, one would lean over and make those daft, cooing noises that people make to babies.

(Well, some people. Not me, I hasten to add.)

One of the footmen came up and muttered in the king's ear. The king nodded, and clapped his hands. Instantly, the violinists put down their bows. The trumpeters, however, leaped importantly to their feet. Slowly, the hubbub of conversation died away.

There was a fanfare – the trumpeters' big moment. The heavy double doors at the opposite end of the great hall swung open ...

And in trooped a load of Fairies!

Now, I don't know how familiar you are with Fairies. You probably think that they are tiny little things with dainty little wings who live under bluebells and use mushrooms for umbrellas when it rains. Well, you're wrong. Oh, they can *make* themselves small if they want to, of course. But most of the time they're human-size, if a little on the short side. They do have wings, though. Their clothes have to have special slits cut in the back for them.

These Fairies were all got up in their best frocks. Net seemed to be the material of choice. They were all cut in the same style – tight bodice, puffy skirt – but in different pastel shades. Their shimmering wings were neatly folded down their backs. They'd all recently had their hair done. It had that just-back-from-the-hairdresser's look.

I did a brief head count as they stood there in ballet positions, with their feet turned out. There were twelve of them. Each held a Wand in one hand and a golden envelope in the other.

With one accord, all the courtiers began to bow and curtsy. Spontaneous applause broke out. The Fairies just stood there in a golden glow, nodding and smiling and graciously acknowledging it all.

With no warning, the sound cut off and the scene froze. I looked sideways at Great-Aunt Angria. Her face was twisted in fury. Choked noises were issuing from her throat. You could almost see smoke coming from her ears. Her hair was on the go again.

'Look at 'em!' she spat. 'Posers! Showin' off in their daft frocks, flauntin' their invites. Hang on, I'll fast-forward this bit.'

She fiddled with her Stick, and the frozen tableau sprang to life again. People began running about at the double, with jerky movements. The Fairies charged up the aisle, vaulted on to the dais and clustered briefly around the cradle before scuttling off and forming a group to one side. One of their members, the one wearing blue, zoomed back to stage centre, waved her Wand around a bit, then sprinted back to join her mates. A yellow one detached herself and did exactly the same thing. Then the lilac, then the white, then the green.

'Hold on,' I said. 'What's going on? I'm losing the plot.'

'They're givin' their daft gifts,' said my auntie, voice

dripping with disgust. 'Grace, charm, a nice singin' voice, kindness to animals, all that malarkey. Ye don't want to hear that. 'Tis borin'. I wants to get to the good bit. Ah, here we are.'

The scene slowed down to normal pace. The sound faded back in.

'... and it is with great pleasure that I give our new baby princess the wonderful gift of Happiness,' the one in lavender was trilling in a high, silvery voice. Rapturous applause from the watching courtiers. She gave a superior smile and tripped off to join her colleagues. And then –

'Now!' shouted Aunt Angry excitedly. 'Watch! Here I come!'

There came a startlingly loud crack of thunder, and the lights dimmed. The huge doors blew open and smashed back against the walls. The crowd gave a united gasp. A footman dropped a tray of ices. Somebody screamed.

And there, framed in the doorway against a background of dark, boiling clouds, was my wicked old auntie. Younger she might have been, but you'd never have known it. She looked exactly the same. I think she was even wearing the same clothes. The only difference was, she wore a traditional tall, pointy witch hat. Her hair flew out from under it, doing the snake routine again. Her temper was obviously up.

At that point, the scene froze again.

'What do ye think?' asked the real, flesh-and-blood version beside me, giving me a sharp nudge in the ribs. 'Impressive or what?'

Personally, I would have lost the hat. They're terribly old-fashioned, witch hats. Hardly anybody wears them any more. But I let it pass.

'Good,' I nodded. 'Very dramatic. Excellent storm.'

'Aye. I knew how to make an entrance, back in them days. People sat up. Watch.'

The scene leaped back into life. Everyone cowered as the star of the show raised her Stick on high. (Yes. Same Stick, in case you're wondering.) Up on the dais, the queen snatched a small bundle from the cradle and clutched it to her chest.

'*So!*' screamed my great-auntie, staring around. People fell over themselves in their efforts to hide. 'Ye're all here, are ye? All present and correct, piggin' out on free drinks and nibbles, all enjoyin' yerselves at the christenin' party! All except me! What's the matter, *Your Majesty*? Gettin' low on *posh gold envelopes*? Run out of *stamps*? *Writer's cramp?*'

'Madam! Please!' That was the king. He was on his feet, face deathly white. 'We thought – we heard – somebody told us you were unwell. Trouble with your feet, we heard. We didn't think you'd be up to it.'

'Aye. I can imagine where *that* little rumour came from,' snarled Aunt Angry, staring hard at the Fairies, who peered haughtily down their noses and huffed and puffed a bit, although it was quite clear that they knew what she meant.

'We didn't want to bother you,' pleaded the king. 'We didn't think it was your sort of thing …'

'And we wanted to use the best golden plates,' added the queen tearfully. 'There are only twelve of them, you see.' Daft woman. She should have kept her mouth shut and left it to her husband.

'*Plates?*' screeched Aunt Angry. Her hair was going bananas again. Her pointy hat was actually jumping up and down on her head. '*Plates? That's* yer excuse? Not enough *plates*? With *your* money? Ye couldn't have gone out *and bought another one?*'

She began hobbling up the aisle. Everyone backed away. Several of the crinolined ladies fainted, but nobody noticed. They were all too busy watching my wicked great-auntie.

'See that? See the way they're backing off?' hissed a voice in my ear. 'By heck, I could show 'em, back then!'

Her Pool version had reached the foot of the dais and stopped. Well, the hair carried on moving, but the rest of her froze. The group of Fairies stopped whispering among themselves, straightened up and watched her carefully.

'I'll give ye *plates*,' hissed the Pool Aunt Angry. Hair thrashing violently, she pointed her Stick at the bundle in the queen's arms. There came another crack of thunder. The bundle let out a single, sad little wail.

'Here is my gift to the baby!' she screamed. She drew herself to her full height – which wasn't very high, but what she lacked in stature she made up in sheer venom. 'Hear this! When she is sixteen years old, she will prick her finger on a spindle – and die! Ha, ha, ha, ha, ha! Oh ha, ha, ha …'

The current Aunt Angry pressed the freeze frame again, cutting her Pool self off mid-cackle and looked at me.

'There,' she said. 'What d'ye think o' that?'

Now, I could understand how she felt, not getting invited and having to listen to all those feeble excuses. But – *die*? That didn't seem right. It didn't seem right at all.

She was still waiting. I had to say something.

'It's – a bit extreme, isn't it?' I said.

'How d'ye mean?'

'Well – you know. Death is so very *final*, don't you think?'

'How should I know? Never been dead.'

'Even so, it was hardly the *baby's* fault –'

'Are ye *criticizin'* me, girl?'

I took one look at her dark, scowling face and gave in. I didn't want a row. I wanted supper.

'It was a very good curse,' I said. 'Brief, but to the point. And you delivered it beautifully.'

'Aye,' growled Aunt Angry. 'It *was* a good curse. And then *she* has to go stickin' 'er blasted oar in and ruinin' it.'

'*She?*'

'Flippin' Rose. The pink one. Hadn't had 'er go yet, see. Well, how was I to know? I thought I'd timed it right.'

'What did she do?'

'I'll show ye.'

Once again, the Pool picture sprang back into life. Everywhere was consternation. People were sobbing. There was more fainting. The queen was in hysterics, the king had his head in his hands. The Fairies were conferring in a huddle. They had their heads together,

70

like a balletic rugby scrum. My Great-Aunt Angria just stood there, smiling a horrible leer of triumph. And then …

The Fairy in pink stepped forward.

'Wait!' she cried. 'Do not despair! I can help!'

Aunt Angry's grin faded.

'Get lost, Rose,' she snarled. 'I'm entitled to give a gift too. If ye don't believe me, look it up in *Ye Booke of Magickal Law*. The curse stands. And there's nothin' ye can do about it.'

'Oh, but you see, there *is*,' said Rose sweetly, tossing back her curls. 'Because *I* haven't given *my* gift yet.'

Hope spread like a great wave around the hall. The queen looked up through her tears. The king stopped wringing his hands. All eyes were on Rose, who was obviously enjoying the attention.

'Much as I'd like to cancel your curse altogether, Angria, the Law won't allow me to do that. But I can soften it a little. *Hear this!*' She stood on tiptoe and raised her Wand. 'The little princess shall not die on her sixteenth birthday. She will merely fall into an enchanted sleep for one hundred years – then be woken by a kiss. And when she wakes, she will be as young and lovely as before!'

There was a long, long silence. Nobody was quite sure how to take this. It was better than death, of course – but a hundred years is a jolly long lie-in by anybody's standards.

Great-Aunt Angry, however, took it very badly indeed. Her eyes burned with green fury. Her lips drew back, exposing her snaggled teeth. Her hair boiled and squirmed. I thought she would explode on the spot.

'So!' she hissed. ''Tis war, is it? Think ye can put one over on me, do ye? Well, ye haven't heard the last o' this. I can wait. Oh, yes. *I can wait!*'

Then she vanished, just like that. There wasn't even a puff of smoke. She just suddenly wasn't there any more.

The surface of the Magic Pool went dark. I looked sideways at a thunderous profile.

'Bad luck,' I sympathized. 'It's rotten, having your curses interfered with, isn't it? Although I really *do* think death was just a wee bit over the top ...'

She wasn't listening.

'Showin' me up in public!' she was muttering, rocking to and fro, mouth working furiously. 'Makin' a laughin' stock o' me. Never been so humiliated in my life!'

'Never mind,' I said, stifling a yawn. I'd had more than enough Pool watching. I couldn't see where it was leading to. 'It's all in the past, isn't it? You must be over it by now, surely?'

'Oh no,' said Aunt Angry softly. 'That's just where ye're wrong, girl. I ain't over it. Not by a long shot.'

She meant it too. I could tell.

'Golly,' I said, looking at my non-existent watch. 'I wonder what the time is? I must say I could do with ...'

'Shut up,' she snapped. 'There's more.'

There was, too.

9. YET MORE MAGIC POOL

It's like people who insist on showing you their home movies. They never know when to stop, do they?

'What – now?' I said.

'Certainly, now. Ye have to know the background, else ye won't know where ye fit in. Here we go. Sixteen years have gone by, right? Got that?'

'Got it,' I sighed, preparing myself for yet more of it. Ralph had gone to sleep, I noticed. I had the feeling he'd watched these particular scenes many, many times before.

This time, the scene in the Magic Pool was very different. It opened on a dark room with low rafters – an attic, by the looks of it. My wicked great-auntie, hatless this time and wearing a long, black dress, was hunched over a spinning-wheel, working away with a big pile of flax at her feet. The attic was windowless, as far as I could see. There was a low door set in one wall.

'That's the wheel you've got on display in the hall, isn't it?' I enquired.

'Aye. Shush. Here she comes.'

'Who?'

'Beauty. Who d'ye think? Pay attention.'

There came the sound of small feet climbing a flight of stairs. The door creaked open and a girl walked in.

She wore a cream satin dress sprinkled with rosebuds. A sparkling tiara topped a head full of golden curls. She had a sweet, heart-shaped face with big blue eyes. I had to admit that she was pretty. Well, more than pretty, actually. She was beautiful.

Now, I normally distrust beautiful people, but funnily enough, I rather liked the look of her – open and natural and friendly. Not at all show-offy, like Scarlettine, for instance.

'Oh!' she said, blue eyes widening in surprise. 'Excuse me. I didn't know there was anyone up here. We were just playing hide-and-seek. I'm so sorry to disturb you.'

'That's all right, little lady,' said my wicked auntie. 'Ye're not bothering me. 'Tain't often I has company.'

The princess's eyes were on the whirring wheel. She seemed fascinated.

'What are you doing?' she asked.

'Spinning, my pretty one,' said Aunt Angry, pulling strands of flax from the pile on the floor and feeding it through the spindle.

'I've never seen anything like it,' said Beauty. 'Is it hard to do?'

'Not at all. Would ye like to try? Shall I show ye?'

'Yes, please. If it's not too much trouble.' She had good manners, as well as good looks.

'Come on over here, then. Sit on the stool. Comfy? Right. Put yer foot on the pedal – so – and hold the thread – so – and the wheel will spin round. See?'

'It's easy!' cried the princess. 'I'm going to ask Mummy and Daddy if I can have one just like it for my next birthday. Are they very expensive? If so, I'll save up all my pocket money and – *Ouch!*' She gave a little gasp, snatched her hand back and stared at her finger. A bright spot of blood appeared on the tip.

'Deary me! What *have* ye gone and done?' enquired Aunt Angry. She just couldn't keep the glee from her voice.

'I've pricked my finger. It hurts! It …'

Suddenly, Beauty went very pale. She stood up, then her knees buckled and she sank to the floor, landing in the pile of flax. She really was very graceful. If it had been me I'd have landed with my head in a bucket.

Great-Aunt Angry let out a great shriek of triumph and the scene went black.

'And there ye have it,' remarked the flesh-and-blood version sitting next to me. 'That happened at exactly three o'clock one hundred years ago Friday.'

'What – this coming Friday?'

'Aye. The thirteenth. Unlucky for some. Lucky for others.'

'So that's when she wakes up, is it? Three o'clock on Friday?'

'That's when she's *due* to wake up,' corrected my

auntie. She gave me a crafty, meaningful look. 'But she won't. Oh no. Nobody gets the better of me. There ain't gonna be no Awakening Day for Beauty.'

'There isn't?'

'Nope. Because I'm gonna put a spanner in the works and stop it happenin'. And ye're gonna help me.'

'I am?'

'Aye. I can't do it on me own. Don't you say a word to no one about this, mind. I'm trustin' you.'

'But we can't,' I said, quite shocked. There are certain rules in Magic. Break them at your peril. 'What about *Ye Booke of Magickal Law*? Rule thirty-two. I learned it for my Grade Three. *Once a spell is cast, it shall only be lifted if the castee so desires it. No direct interference is permitted by another party except by prior arrangement.*'

'And what d'ye think she done to my curse, then? Rose?'

'Ah, but that was different. She didn't *lift* your spell. She just *changed* it a little. And she was allowed to do that because she hadn't had her turn and the Law says –'

'Enough!' shouted my auntie, banging her Stick on the floor. Her hair began to squirm about restlessly. 'Don't ye go quotin' the Law at me, girl!'

'But it states quite clearly that no interference is permitted –'

'No direct interference. *Direct*. It don't say nowhere that I can't interfere *indirectly*, do it? And that's where you come in.'

'I do?'

'Aye. Ye're gonna be my eyes and legs, see.'

'I am?'

'Yep. Now, listen carefully. Here's what ye got to do.'
And she told me.

There was quite a lot of it, so I'll sum it up for you.

The Twelve Fairies, I learned, were now all retired and living in a luxurious mansion known as the Pink House. Where? Well, where do you think? Fairyland, of course. That lies somewhere over the rainbow, I gathered. Great-Aunt Angry seemed a bit vague about that. Anyway, the Pink House was heavily guarded with spells and nobody could gain access without an invitation. My job, she told me, was to go along and spy. I was to snoop about and find out as many details as I could about what was planned for the forthcoming Awakening Day and report back to her. She would then take the appropriate action, whatever that meant.

There seemed a few holes in this, and I said so.

'How will I get there?' I enquired. 'The Pink House, Fairyland, Somewhere Over the Rainbow. Bit of a vague address, isn't it?'

'Ye can leave that to me. I'll get ye there.'

'But how am I supposed to get in? If it's guarded with spells, like you say?'

'Ah,' said Aunt Angry. 'Thought ye'd ask that. Take a look at this. They're all over the place. Saw this one in the post-office window, when I posted me letter to yer ma.'

She fumbled around in her layers of woollies, withdrew a pink folded piece of paper and held it out. I opened it out. There were butterflies in the border and three lines of silvery writing.

'*Wanted,*' I read out loud. '*Extra kitchen staff to help prepare for forthcoming Awakening Day Grand Celebration*

Party. Good wages. Applicants will be expected to live in for the duration. Apply in person to the Pink House, Fairyland.'

'Ye can keep that. Stick it in yer pocket. Ye can wave it about when ye go for the job.'

'What makes you think they'll take me on? They might have enough staff already,' I pointed out.

'Well, ye'll just have to use yer powers of persuasion, won't ye? I dunno, kids today, all want spoon feedin'. I said I'll get ye there. It's up to you then.'

'But what if they don't believe me?'

'*Make* 'em believe ye. Act humble. Nothin' to it.'

'Well, if it's that easy, why don't you do it yourself? You could go in disguise, couldn't you?'

'What, with my feet?' Her face darkened. 'Anyway, I can't get in. Not allowed into Fairyland. I'm blacklisted. I've tried, but I always get stopped at the border. I can't even watch 'em in the Pool. They always knows when I tries a bit o' spyin'. Got all these spells of protection set up. *Ye've* got to go.'

'I don't know,' I said doubtfully.

'What d'ye mean, ye don't know?'

'I don't know how I feel about all this. Look, don't get me wrong. I know what it's like to want revenge. But ...'

'But what?'

'Well – what happens to the princess?'

'Nothin'. Oh, she won't *die*, if that's what ye're gettin' at.'

'What, then?'

'She'll just carry on sleepin'. For ever.'

I thought about this. There didn't seem much difference.

'But isn't that a bit unfair? She seems harmless enough ...'

I trailed off. Great-Aunt Angry was scowling at me, her face a mask of disgust.

'Whose side are ye on, Wilma?' she asked cuttingly. 'Ye're talkin' sentimental claptrap. Twelve flippin' hoity-toity, do-goodin' *Fairies* got the better of me. Me, yer own flesh an' blood. And ye're worried about a stranger what ye've never even met. Ain't ye ever heard about blood bein' thicker than water? Ye come from a long line of wicked queens, girl. Ye've a proud tradition to uphold.'

'But —'

'And don't talk to me about fairness, neither. Where does it say life has to be fair? 'Tain't fair that I never got invited to all them family christenin's an' birthdays and weddin's an' anniversaries an' welcome-'ome parties ye been enjoyin' over the years.'

'Oh, but I'm sure you were, Great-Aunt Angria. The post is so unreli—'

'Shut up. *I'm* talkin' now. I'm tellin' ye what ain't fair. 'Tain't fair that I never got to be Queen o' the Night. I was better suited to it than Grimelza. My Power was the stronger. But I was born five minutes — a lousy five minutes, mind — after her, so she got the job. Where's the fairness in that?'

I thought about this. I've had my share of losing out to older sisters. I knew how she felt.

'So,' she said. 'What's it to be, Wilma? Can I count on you or not?'

Well, what was I to say?

'Yes,' I said, with a defeated sigh. 'You can. I'll do my best, Great-Aunt Angria.'

'Good. Ralph! Wake up! Take 'er to 'er bedroom. I'll stay down here for a bit.'

That was that, then. I was committed.

10. MY BAD NIGHT

Goody. Wouldn't you just know it? My bedroom only turned out to be right at the very top of the tallest turret in the castle. I followed Ralph up a zillion stairs, trying not to puff too much. Not only was I breathless, I was faint from lack of food. Great-Aunt Angry seemed to have forgotten all about her promise of supper. Too busy brooding about injustice, I suppose. I had left her down in the dungeons, rocking and mumbling and fiddling with her hair.

'Is there anything to eat in this place?' I croaked, as we rounded yet another bend.

'Not a lot,' Ralph took great pleasure in telling me. 'Mishtresh is a frugal eater. Gruel or porridge. That'sh the choishe.'

'I'll pass,' I said firmly. Gruel or porridge, my foot. I do like my food. Some visit this was turning out to be.

'If you'd have thought, you could have brought along a little bashket,' said Ralph, stopping suddenly in his tracks so that I nearly ran into him. His voice had taken on a weird, dreamy quality. 'A nishe little bashket with a checked cloth on the top. Filled with goodiesh. Pink cakesh and honey and a bottle of wine for Granny.'

'What?' I snapped. What was the wretched animal going on about now?

'I was jusht shaying you could have brought your own little −'

'Yes, yes, all right, I *heard* what you said. I didn't understand it, that's all. What's my grandma got to do with it?'

'Nothing.' He went all sulky. 'Forget I shaid it, all right?'

'No, no, please explain. My grandma, as you well know, is the ex-Queen of the Night. Right now she's attending a Gypsy Convention in another dimension, living on camp-fire food. What would she want with pink cakes in a nice little basket?'

'Doeshn't matter.'

'No, really, I insist. Do I look like a nice little basket sort of person? You keep making all these incomprehensible remarks. Is it a Wolf Thing? Or are you just plain, barking mad?'

'I shaid forget it! You wouldn't undershtand anyway!' snapped Ralph, and stalked on up the stairs, very put out indeed.

He really was *very* odd. I made a mental note to ask Aunt Angry about him sometime.

When we finally reached the room that was to be mine, I was past caring what it was like. Just as well, really. It was a small, bare circular turret room. There were four things in it. No, five:

A bed (narrow, thin mattress; single sheet)
A wardrobe (small, wooden, empty)
My trunk (sitting slap bang in the middle of the floor.
    Don't know how it got there.)
Cobwebs
Cold air

'I hope you'll be comfortable,' sneered Ralph, lying through his fangs.

'Why, thank you,' I said, hurling myself on the bed, which was so hard I nearly did myself a severe injury. 'Most kind. Ouch.'

'Should you require anything elshe, I'm afraid you'll just have to get off your big, fat b— ed and get it yourshelf. I shall be otherwishe engaged.' He licked his lips triumphantly.

'Which is it? Nice bone in the kennel or baying at the moon?'

'Ho, ho. You think you're sho funny, don't you?' he growled.

'I *know* I'm funny. Anyway, I'm tired. Go away.'

'I musht shay you're not what I was ecshpecting. Frankly, you've proved a big dishappointment sho far.'

'Out!' I ordered, pointing sternly. Back chat from a

83

talking wolf, indeed. Whatever was the world coming to? 'Now! Bad wolf! Shall I get a rolled-up newspaper? Shall I?'

He stood eyeing me, teeth bared to the gums. I could see he was fighting down the urge to let go and really, *really* bark at me. He didn't, though. He just backed out, all long and low and stiff-legged, then turned and streaked down the stairs. There was a distant howl. Afterwards, silence.

The first thing I did was go to my trunk, take out everything edible and eat all of it. Well, almost all of it. As I've already mentioned, one of the packets of chocolate biscuits had been gnawed open and they were all melted together and covered in cat hairs. But I ate the rest, following them up with the doughnuts and mince pies. I saved the box of chocolate eclairs in case of emergency. And one doughnut and a couple of sugar lumps for Denzil. I'd probably regret not saving more, but hey! I was hungry, right?

I brushed the crumbs off the sheet – not that it mattered, it was so dirty anyway. Next I went and had another rummage in the trunk. Was it my imagination or was it getting even colder? Not that I could do much to warm myself up. My hot-water bottle had more punctures than a colander. Denzil really had done a lot of damage.

I pulled out Graham my frog, my guitar and my MoBall, all of which I took back to the bed. I flopped down, pulling my still damp cloak around me. My breath made little puffs in the air. It *was* getting colder, no doubt about it.

There came a scratching at the small high window. A soft, insistent sort of scratching that was obviously intended for sinister effect.

I didn't even bother to look. We were hundreds of metres up from the ground. It stood to reason there was no one there. No one worth bothering with, anyway. Another flipping ghost, probably. If I ignored it, it would give up and go away.

I took my MoBall out of its velvet pouch and cradled it in my hands.

I haven't told you about my new MoBall, have I? It's great. I was quite pleased with my last Crystal Ball, which had all the usual functions – long-range audio facilities; past, present or future options and so on and so forth. I say *pleased*. Well, I was until the power ran down and I read the small print about it needing to rest for a month after heavy usage. What good is that?

This one was much better. Smaller, neater; good, crisp picture, and back-up batteries.

I love using it. I decided to give Mother a try. Just to tell her I was safe in bed – well, sitting on it cross-legged – and not to worry.

I said the appropriate mystic word, which I won't give out to you, if you don't mind. Mother's very fussy about who gets her private Ball word. You can't blame her. She spends all her time on the Ball as it is. She's very popular and gets invited to a lot of boring official functions.

It was engaged. Oh well. I could always use emergency override. I hadn't tried that yet.

I made the appropriate mystic sign. Instantly, my MoBall began to flash on and off and set up a high, tinny sort of wail. Hmm. Interesting. There was a moment or two of this, then it stopped and I found myself gazing into Mother's frantic face. She was still in the Coach, of course, it being the middle of the night.

'What?' she gasped. 'What is it? Wilma, is that you? What's the matter? What's happened?'

'Not a lot,' I said. 'I got in all right. I'm in bed.'

'But – you used the emergency override! I was just on the Ball talking to Daddy when there came this awful wailing! I nearly jumped out of my *skin,* darling!'

'Sorry,' I said, hurt. 'I thought I'd say goodnight. Don't you want me to?'

'Well – of course I do. Just don't do it again, my nerves are in shreds as it is. So. Are you all settled in?'

'Oh yes.'

'I see you haven't brushed your hair. Aunt Angria must have thought you were a fright.'

'No,' I said. 'She didn't. She's got frightening hair problems of her own.'

'Yes, come to think of it, I *do* remember the hair. But how is she otherwise? Did she like the presents?'

'She stuffed the gout cream down the sofa and smashed the photo on the floor.'

'No change there, then,' said Mother with a little sigh. 'Mind out for glass in your feet. Anything else to report?'

'There's a talking wolf here,' I said. 'I think he might be mad. He's called Ralph.'

'Oh, that's nice. Look, darling, I don't want to rush you, but …'

'I thought you wanted me to talk to you.'

'I do, I do.'

86

'But you're acting like you're not interested.'

'Oh, I am, I am. What is it Aunt Angria wants you to do, anyway?'

'I can't tell you that. It's private.'

There was a little pause.

'Did you brush your teeth?' enquired Mother.

'I'm going to. How was Frostia, by the way?' (Notice how brilliant I am at changing the subject.)

'Don't ask,' groaned Mother. 'Surrounded by twenty-five million ice blocks and a work-force of cowboy Inuits who've gone on strike because she won't pay extra to provide them with waterproof mittens and tea-making facilities.'

(Cowboy Inuits, eh? The mind boggles. Do they wear Stetsons with their furry anoraks?)

'Poor darling,' Mother went on. 'The stress is really beginning to tell. I left her in bed in that horrid little temporary igloo she's living in with a comforting iced drink.'

'Still no news of Uncle Bacchus?'

'No. Nobody can raise him. I'm getting really worried now. And on top of everything, Daddy tells me that Denzil has gone missing and Mrs Pudding won't even *think* about cooking until he's found. And you know how fussy Daddy is when we eat out. He keeps complaining that the vegetables aren't organic.'

'Really?' I said. 'Denzil missing, eh? Dear me.'

I felt guilty. Not only had I stolen him, I'd now gone and lost him. For ever, by the looks of it.

The scratching came at the window again.

'Oh, shut up,' I snapped.

'Pardon?'

'Not you. There's a ghost or something tapping on the window.'

'Oh, right. Well, look, I'd really better go. Bacchus might be trying to get through. Kiss?' Mother's mouth screwed up and she pecked the air.

'Kiss,' I said, with a little sigh.

'Take care, darling.'

There was a little green whirlpool effect, and her image was sucked away, leaving the MoBall plain again, like a glass paperweight.

I practised my guitar then, for two whole minutes. Alvis says you have to do it regularly. My music is very important to me. I can nearly play the chord of C now and I've only been learning a few weeks. (Alvis is teaching me. Did I mention that?)

As soon as my fingers were sore, I lay down with my head on Graham and went to sleep, straight away. I was *that* tired.

In the night, I dreamed a lot of things. I dreamed that a load of wailing ghosts danced in formation at the foot of my bed. I dreamed that the various suits of armour dotted around the castle formed a line and came clanking up the stairs and through my room before vanishing into my wardrobe. I dreamed that the door knob slowly turned and the door opened and there was no one outside. I dreamed that a couple of weird marks I had noticed on the plaster turned into eyes, and one of them winked at me. I dreamed I heard echoing footsteps, screams, and peals of mocking laughter coming from down below in the castle. I dreamed I heard sharp cracklings and rappings coming from my trunk, which I knew for a fact didn't have any wrapping paper in it, ha, ha (joke). I dreamed I lay on a guitar and it hurt. I dreamed I heard the phantom organist again. I dreamed I was in the desert with a mouthful of sand.

Then I dreamed that something leaped on my stomach. I jerked awake, spitting out frog stuffing and let out a small scream, only to find that I wasn't dreaming at all!

It was Denzil! He was all purry and dribbly and pleased to see me. I offered him the doughnut and the sugar lumps but he turned his nose up. I had a feeling he'd already eaten. I knew there were mice in the castle and he was hiccuping a lot.

But I hugged him anyway.

Then I wrapped my cloak around me and went back to sleep, where I dreamed that a phantom with glowing red eyes walked through the wall and pinched my sheet.

Some night.

11. SOMEWHERE OVER THE RAINBOW

I could tell you about the following morning, I suppose. About how I woke in the cold light of dawn, freezing, with the imprint of a guitar in my back, only to find that my sheet had, in fact, gone missing. There was no sign of Denzil either. What a fickle friend he was proving to be.

I could tell you about how I got up and ate the emergency chocolate eclairs, slipped my Wand and my MoBall into my cloak pocket (I like to be prepared, as you know), clumped down the zillion steps that I'd toiled up only a few short hours before, then spent the best part of an hour wandering crossly through a maze of passageways, looking for breakfast.

I could tell you about how I finally came across a

squalid, empty kitchen with a single bowl of tepid, lumpy porridge set on the table. About how horrible it was. About how I ate it anyway.

I could tell you about the calendar on the wall. Great-Aunt Angry certainly didn't have much of a social life. It was empty, apart from a red ring circling Friday the thirteenth. Inside the ring, inscribed in shaky letters, were the significant words: *Awakening Day!!*

I could tell you about how Ralph came in through the special wolf flap set in the kitchen door. I noticed him giving it a suspicious sniff. I suspected that Denzil had acquainted himself with that particular facility.

'Ready?' asked Ralph, giving me a Look. He was particularly stand-offish and sneery this morning, after our sharp words of the night before. 'She ish waiting.'

'Where?'

'In Her room. Follow me.'

Goody. Stairs again. We climbed them in chilly silence.

Aunt Angry was sitting in her armchair, which was back in its usual place. She looked better this morning. Brighter. In fact, there was a definite air of excitement about her.

'There ye are. About bloomin' time,' she said. Adding: 'Sleep all right?'

'No,' I said. 'A phantom took my sheet.'

'Ah. Diddums.'

'Actually,' I said, 'I'm getting rather fed up with the ghosts around here. They're wasting their time on me. I'd be grateful if you'd pass the message on.'

'Fair enough,' said Aunt Angry. 'They're a bit excited because ye're new. I'll 'ave a word.'

91

'How are your feet this morning?' I asked. I'd just noticed she had her shoes on.

'I dunno. No worse. Bit better, I s'pose.'

'Did you use Mother's cream?'

'Tried a bit. Didn't hurt. Anyway, what we wastin' time for? Go and stand in the Ring. I've drawn it already. I noticed last night ye can't draw a decent Magic Ring for toffee. Wobbled all over the shop. What do they teach you girls these days?'

I looked at where she was pointing. A pale green circle glowed faintly on the floor over by the window, through which I could see the beginnings of sunrise. Mother was home, then.

'Go on, get in. What ye waitin' for?'

'Aren't you going to give me anything?' I asked.

'Like what?'

'I don't know. Your blessing? A Magical amulet for protection? A cloak of invisibility, perhaps? Ruby slippers? Some instructions about what to do when I get there? Or how I get back?'

'I don't do blessin's. Cursin's my speciality. And ye don't need none of the other stuff. These is common Fairies ye're dealin' with. *Fairies*, not *Faeries*. I should hope ye could cope.'

'*You* didn't,' I muttered under my breath.

'What? What did ye say?'

'Nothing.'

'Good. Got yer Wand?'

'Of course,' I said, patting my pocket. 'Never go anywhere without it.'

'There ye go, then. Just keep yer eyes and ears open,

blend into the background and find out what ye can. Ralph'll get ye home when ye're done. Today's Wednesday. Tomorrow night at sunset, that's when I'll expect ye back. That should give me plenty of time to make me preparations. Come on, come on, don't 'ang about. The timing's critical. Go on, Ralph. I knows ye don't want to, but this is business. Get in that Ring and *sit*!'

'Go on,' I taunted him. 'Time for walkies.'

He curled a lip at me and bristled a bit before he slunk unwillingly into the Ring with his ears down. I followed.

'Here we go,' said my wicked great-auntie. 'Don't let me down, mind.'

And she twisted the knob of her Stick. There came the bang, the flash ...

... and I found myself standing in a haze of greenish smoke, on the edge of a wood. The sun was shining. The sky was blue. Birds twittered in the trees. Butterflies buttered about. A dear little bunny rabbit was playing near by. It took one look at Ralph and shot off into the undergrowth, white tail bobbing.

There was a tinkling stream, a rustic bridge and clumps of pretty flowers nodding in the warm breeze. Before me, three cute little lambs gambolled in a field of green, green grass. In the distance was a large house with pointy turrets, surrounded by high walls. The roofs were made of gold. They flashed in the sun. Everything else, including the gates, was pink.

So this was Fairyland. It wasn't really my bag. Far too twee – though I had to admit it was pretty in a dinglydellish sort of way. The only thing that spoiled the perfection of it all was the circle of charred, blackened grass in which we stood. Poisonous-looking toadstools, thistles, clumps of Deadly Nightshade and stinging nettles formed the circumference. Our Faerie Ring. Note the spelling.

'We've made a bit of a mess,' I remarked to Ralph. That was an understatement. Our horrible Ring was a complete blight on the landscape. It was like a dark coffee stain on a pristine tablecloth. The surrounding trees seemed to be struggling to keep their branches away from it.

Ralph didn't reply. His yellow eyes were glued to the gambolling lambs. He was drooling quite heavily, I noticed. A low rumbling issued from his throat.

'I suppose I'd best make a move, then. Are you coming?'

'No,' said Ralph distractedly. He was slowly beginning to sink into a crouch. 'I'm shtaying here to guard the Ring. You're on your own.'

'Fair enough,' I said, shrugging. 'See you.'

'Yeah, yeah. Catch you later. When you get to the cottage.'

'What?'

'I mean the Ring. I'll shee you back here, at the Ring.'

'You said cottage. What cottage? What are you talking about, *cottage*?'

He didn't reply. The lambs were playing chase-my-tail around a clump of buttercups. I left him to it and set off across the dewy grass. Mad as a hatter, that one.

A short time later, I stood gazing up at the pink gates of the Pink House. I knew right away I was being watched. The air hummed with Magic. I could taste it. Spells of Protection and Defence had been woven here. The owners obviously didn't believe in taking chances.

There was a Magicom unit fitted to one of the gateposts. It was a small plastic box with a grille which you speak into. Pretty standard, except that this one was pink. I stood on tiptoe and spoke into it.

"Ello?' I said, in what I assumed was a maid's accent. Humble anxiety was the effect I was aiming for. I think I did it rather well. 'Anyone at 'ome?'

'Password, please,' came a high, polite, silvery voice from out of the box.

'Oi don't know no paaassword,' I squeaked. 'Oi just come about the job, please'm. Oi seen this advertisement.' I pulled the folded piece of paper from my pocket, flapped it about a bit, and dropped a little curtsy, for good measure.

There was a short pause. A piece of tinkly music, heavy on bells, faded in then out again. Then the voice said:

'Name?'

'Eliza 'Iggins, mum, if you please.'

There was another pause and another snatch of music before the voice said:

'Report to the kitchen. Chef will see you there. Follow the wall around to the back of the house. There's a tradesman's entrance.'

'Thank ye kindly, mum,' I said, and dropped another curtsy. So far, so good.

I followed the wall around. It had spikes on the top, I noticed. They had been painted pink and had ivy twined around them, but they were still spikes. I found the tradesman's entrance — a small, humble door tucked away behind the dustbins. I gave a gentle tap.

It opened straight away and I found myself gazing down into the upturned face of a kitchen leprechaun. He had pointy ears and a long beard. The top of his head was on a level with the area I refer to as my waist. I knew he was a kitchen leprechaun because:

1. *He was dressed from head to toe in green, apart from his apron.*
2. *His hat had a sprig of shamrock jauntily tucked into the brim.*
3. *He was up to the armpits in dough.*

'Top o' the marnin' to ye, darlin',' he greeted me cheerily. 'I won't shake yer hand, 'tis in the middle o' kneadin' the dough I am. Ye're after work, so I hear.'

'Yes, sir, that's roight, sir, Oi am, sir, if you please,' I said, and gave him a shy curtsy.

'Well, we can do with the extra pair o' hands, to be sure. And less o' the sirs. We're all on first-name terms round here. Apart from Chef, of course. I'm Shaun. What shall I be after callin' ye, darlin'?'

'Eliza 'Iggins if you please, Mr Shaun sir.'

'Well, 'tis glad I am to be seein' ye, young Eliza. We're that busy, Chef's tearin' his hair out. Come along in and I'll take ye to him. Don't be put off, now. His bark's worse than his bite.'

And he turned and set off at a fast trot. I hurried along behind, mentally congratulating myself on my incredible role-playing. So far, so good.

12. THE KITCHENS

I couldn't believe the racket in the kitchen, which seemed to be staffed almost exclusively by leprechauns who are, as everyone knows, noisy little blighters. They're hard workers, though, I'll give you that. They were everywhere, rushing about on their little green legs and bellowing at each other.

'Hey, Cormac! Bring us that sack o' sugar!'

'Mary! What have ye done with the milk jug?'

'Flour needed over here! How many more times?'

'Mind what ye're doin' with that rollin' pin, Brodie! Nearly had me head off!'

'Make way! Logs! More logs comin' through!'

The kitchen fumed with rich, sweet aromas – toffee, fudge, chocolate, hot strawberry sauce, warm treacle.

One entire wall was lined with braziers and ovens, which were being loaded with trays full of uncooked pies, tarts, cakes and doughnuts. It seemed that the Fairies had a sweet tooth. (Or should that be sweet teeth?)

At one end, there was a great stone chimney full of crackling logs which was attended by a team of sweating leprechauns in soot-stained tunics. A huge cauldron was suspended on a hook. By the smell, it was full of bubbling chocolate.

Three tiny females wearing embroidered green skirts and green kerchiefs were perched on stools over a great, marble slab, dementedly rolling out huge sheets of pastry. The rolling pins were big and heavy and their faces were scarlet with effort. That didn't stop them talking, though. Or shrieking, more like.

'Hey, Bridget! How's that no good husband of yours? Does he have a job yet?'

'Sure and so he has, Maeve. He's after bein' a postman.'

'Is that right? And there was you sayin' he couldn't walk as far as the kitchen sink to wash a cup. Hey, Liam! More flour needed over here!'

In the midst of all this chaos stood a tall, thin man in whites. This must be the chef. He had a thin little moustache and a goatee beard. A tall hat stood on his head. Every so often it banged into the bunches of onions and dried herbs hanging from the greasy rafters. He was waving his arms around, screeching louder than anybody.

'*Non!*' he was shrieking. 'Not like *zat*! Ze cherry 'as to go in ze *meeddle* of ze cake! Ze *meeddle*! Not to ze 'ow-you-say *side*, yeu *stupeed*!'

Shaun trotted over to him and pulled at his sleeve. Chef frowned and bent down. Shaun shouted in his ear and pointed at me. Chef rolled his eyes and clutched at his hat in exasperation. Then he gave a huge, overdone, theatrical sigh and came marching over, Shaun scuttling along at his side.

'This is Chef Basin, Eliza,' said Shaun. 'Curtsy nicely.'

I curtsied nicely to hide my confusion. Chef Basin! I knew that name. Aunt Angry had mentioned him. He used to cook soufflés back at the Ancestral Halls when she and Grandma were girls. What a coincidence! Ironic, too. I mean, he used to work for us and now he'd gone over to the opposition. He certainly kept his age well. Must be all that arm-waving and shouting. Good exercise, I suppose.

'Bah San!' said Chef Basin, sharply.

What? Could he speak Chinese?

'Sorry, Chef,' said Shaun cheerfully. 'I just can't seem to get it.'

'Ees *Bah San*. Zat is ze way my name is 'ow-you-say, prrronounced. Not zis silly way yeu say, baysun. I am *Monsieur Bah San*. 'Ow much more times I tell yeu zis?'

'I know, I know. I'll get it in time. Anyway, this here is Eliza. She's come about the job. Say hello to Chef Basin, Eliza.'

'*Bah San!*' screamed Chef. '*Bah San*, yeu stupeed!'

'Yes, sir, please, sir,' I said, and dropped another humble curtsy. I'm glad I don't have to be humble in real life. Too hard on the knees.

''Ave yeu wairked in keetchen beforrre?' barked Chef Basin, fixing me with a steely glare.

100

'Oh, yes sir, please sir, Oi 'ave, sir.'

Well, I had. As you know, I often help Mrs Pudding.

'Zen what aire yeu waiting for? Get ze apron on and start!'

'Please sir, what start sir, what sir, please?' I trilled.

'*Zat!*' screeched Chef Basin, pointing to a sink with a huge mountain of greasy pots and pans. 'Start *zat*. Now, do not bozzer me. Hey, yeu! Paddy! Mind what you do wiz zat marrrzipan, yeu *stupeeed*!' And he raced away, arms whirling like windmills.

Shaun hooked an apron off a hook and handed it to me with a wink.

'There ye are, Eliza. Who's a lucky girl, then? Ye've got the job. Boiling water's in the buckets over by the fire. Soap under the sink. See ye later.'

And off he went, leaving me with about three days' worth of washing-up.

Well, you've washed up. You know what it's like. I confess I didn't, not until then. Washing-up is not one of my culinary skills. I excel in the mixing and tasting and spilling things on the floor bit of cooking. You can keep the rest of it. What do we pay the servants for?

Anyway, I won't bore you with the details. Just think grease, steam, grease, steam and more grease and you'll get the picture. What I did that *was* interesting, though, was listen. Leprechauns are shocking gossips. In no time at all, I learned the following things:

1. Yes, there was indeed a celebration planned for the day after tomorrow. It was clearly a big deal.

Big banquet, champagne, live music, squeakers, fancy hats, fireworks, bells ringing out all over Fairyland, the full works, no expense spared.

2. Bridget's husband was one lazy leprechaun. I hoped he didn't come delivering in our dimension. The post is bad enough already.

3. The Twelve Fairies were terribly excited about the forthcoming Awakening Party, as it was generally referred to. It was the first big do they had had in years, apparently.

4. Shaun was married to Mary and they had nine children at home who right now would be running rings around the babysitter.

5. The Awakening itself would be watched live in the lounge on the Magic Screen, whatever that was. Champagne corks would be popped at the moment of the Kiss.

6. There was a Prince involved. His name was Brett. He'd been already picked out.

7. He wasn't bad-looking, according to Maeve.

8. The smell of sugar makes you sick after a while.

9. So does washing-up.

I also learned why the Pink House was pink. It had been the Pink Fairy (Rose) who had cast the Sleep Spell that had softened my wicked great-auntie's curse all those years ago. As a reward for this achievement, she got to choose the colour scheme. Amazing how much you can find out if you keep your mouth closed and your ears open.

All day I stood there, up to my armpits in greasy water, trying to cope as well as I could despite my lack of expertise. The leprechauns kept idly chucking more dirty plates, pots and utensils into the water. Every time they did so, I got splashed. I felt like chucking them back, and had to keep reminding myself that I was humble Eliza, who wouldn't say boo to a goose. The draining board was piled so high it had nearly reached critical mass, but I couldn't stop to deal with that because, if I did, the sink got so full I couldn't even get to the water. It was a nightmare. Nobody seemed to stop for lunch. And throughout it all, Chef Basin ran around the place throwing mega temper tantrums that involved a lot of flying forks.

Funny. I had always imagined Fairy kitchens to be serene, cosy little places where they would sit around a prettily laid table sipping dandelion tea and nibbling at frosted fairy cakes. You live and learn.

I thought the day would never end – but it did. At sunset, a siren went off and everyone downed tools and took off their aprons. Some fresh leprechauns – the night cleaning squad, I suppose – came trooping in armed with brooms and scrubbing brushes and began hosing the place down.

'Ye can stop now, Eliza,' said Mary. 'Give me yer apron. My, what a mess ye've made of yerself, darlin'. Ye're soaked. Have ye not done the washin'-up before?'

'Sorry, mum, please, mum, Oi'll do it better tomorrow.'

'There's a good girl. Come with me, I'll get ye a bite to eat. Afterwards I'll show ye to yer room. Ye'll have to be up good and early in the marnin'. Did ye bring an overnight bag?'

Ah. I hadn't thought of that.

'Wicked robbers pinched me basket, mum, on the way 'ere, mum,' I lied, putting a little wobble in my voice. I was getting to be quite an actress. I felt so sorry for myself I almost *did* cry.

'Tut tut,' went Mary. 'And in Fairyland, too. What a world it is, to be sure. Now, what do ye fancy? We're all having leprechaun broth. Will ye have a drop?'

'Yes, mum, please, mum, thank you, mum,' I nodded.

I had three big bowlfuls – and very nice it was too.

Some time later, I sat cross-legged on the narrow bunk in an attic room. Princess or maid, I always seem to be given the attic room, do you notice? Oh well. It was only for the one night. And it was a better attic room than the one in Starkacre Hall. At least it was clean, and there was a blanket and pillow on the bunk. Two sheets, too. There was even a bedside table on which somebody had thoughtfully placed a stub of a candle and a box of matches. Just as well. It was dark now. Mother must be in the Night Coach.

I reached into my pocket and pulled out my MoBall. Time to give her another flash. She was probably dying to hear from me.

She was engaged again. I was just about to use the emergency override, when her image floated into view.

'Don't do it, Wilma!' she commanded. 'You were going to, weren't you? Lucky I noticed you trying to get through. What is it you want, darling? Be quick.'

She wasn't in the Night Coach, as I expected. She was in her office back at the Ancestral Halls. This was highly unusual.

'Why aren't you on the Round?' I asked. 'Who's Bringing the Night?'

'Gloria's doing it, as a favour.'

Gloria is the Queen of Storms (aka Rumbleguts).

'Why?'

'Because I've got several emergencies on my hands, Wilma. I can't do everything.'

'Like what?'

'Darling, do I *have* to tell you now? This isn't a good time to talk. While I'm talking to you, at least three other people are trying to get through.'

'I want to know,' I said stubbornly. 'I'm part of this family too. What emergencies?'

'All right! If you really want to know. We've had another postcard from Scarlettine. Her ship's been captured by pirates, can you believe? Poor, poor darling. They made her captain walk the plank. And they'd only just got engaged, too.'

'Only the captain?' I asked, disappointed. If it had been Scarlettine walking the plank, that *would* have been cause for celebration. Mother chose to ignore this.

'And I had Maud on the Ball just now. Your Grandma's gone all native. She's learning flamenco dancing, apparently. They can't get her to bed at night. She's dressing most unsuitably for her age and talking about getting her ears pierced. I think they're feeling the strain. It's such a *little* caravan. Mind you, Maud's brought it on herself. I did tell her that Mama can be trying.'

'Any news of Alvis?' I asked.

'No. Daddy's very worried about the tomatoes. The show is next week and he's had two tonnes of mulch delivered and nobody to help him spread it the way he likes it.'

'Has Mrs Pudding found Denzil?' I enquired casually.

'No, that's another thing. It was bread and dripping for dinner tonight. She's out in the grounds now, rattling his biscuit tin.'

'I expect he'll come,' I said. 'He always comes for his biscuits.' He'd have a job. His biscuits were a zillion miles and four dimensions away.

'But the worst news of all is Uncle Bacchus.'

'What about him? Have you found him yet?'

'No, that's the problem. I was so worried when I got back this morning, exhausted though I was, I didn't bother with bed. I went straight to his island in person. And he's not there. No note or anything. The castle was wide open. Anyone could have walked in.'

'Any signs of a break-in?'

'I don't know. It's always so untidy it's hard to be sure. I did notice an overturned chair. And a half-eaten kebab. Oh dear.'

She really sounded upset. Uncle Bacchus is her adopted brother and she's fond of him. Well, we all are.

'He'll be all right,' I said. 'I'm sure of it. By the way, you'll never believe where I'm calling from? I'm in Fairy—'

'Darling, I don't want to rush you, but *please* get off the Ball. We'll speak again, when things aren't quite so fraught, yes? Are you having a lovely time?'

'Nope,' I said. 'Not really. Cheerio.' And I cut the connection.

I put the MoBall back into its pouch, unlaced my

boots, blew out the candle and lay down on the bed, wishing I'd thought to bring Graham. And my guitar. I was supposed to practise every night. I didn't want my C to fall behind. Mind you, my hands were so sore with all the washing-up that I doubted whether I could play it anyway.

My last thought before dropping off to sleep was of Denzil. I felt terribly guilty about him. I did hope he was all right.

13. TWELVE GOOD FAIRIES

I awoke to the horrible sound of a clanging bell and running footsteps. I groaned and sat up, rubbing my eyes. Morning already? It didn't seem possible.

Still. The great thing about going to bed in your clothes is that it doesn't take long to get up. Yawning, I dragged myself down to the kitchen, hoping for breakfast. No such luck. The leprechauns were already at their posts and Chef Basin was getting stuck into his first major tantrum of the day. To my horror, I saw that the sink was filling up with dirty dishes.

I found a clean apron and was just dragging myself across when Chef Basin spotted me.

'Yeu!' he screamed. 'Go to ze lounge and peek up ze dirty crocks. At ze double!'

'Take the trolley, darlin',' advised Shaun, already elbow deep in dough. He pointed to a metal trolley standing by the door. 'Through the door, along the corridor, last door on the left. Knock before you go in. And curtsy nicely.'

I took the trolley, manhandled it through the door and set off down the corridor, which was painted pink. There were twelve simpering portraits in golden frames lining the walls. I recognized the twelve Fairies from their guest appearance in the Magic Pool. I would have studied them properly, but I was too busy fighting with the trolley. It was like all trolleys in the known universe. The four wheels just wouldn't co-operate. Even in Fairyland it isn't possible to get one that will go straight.

I finally reached the last door on the left. Guess what colour it was painted? Right.

I gave a humble little tap.

'Enter,' trilled a voice. In I went, pushing the infuriating trolley before me.

The (pink!) room I found myself standing in was horribly hot and smelled of old roses. In the centre, an obstacle course had been laid out – padded footstools, bags of knitting, magazine racks and a dozen low tables on which dirty breakfast dishes had been dumped alongside a great many vases of flowers and overflowing bowls of fruit.

Chintzy pink sofas and armchairs were arranged facing a blank, white wall. Funny. You would think they would have been facing the hearth, in which a roaring fire blazed and crackled away. Over it was an elegant mantelpiece containing dozens of photographs. Hanging above it was a large, handsomely framed mirror. Another wall was taken up with a large picture window framed with pink velvet curtains, overlooking rolling green lawns.

I couldn't work out why one wall was white when every other wall was painted pink and cluttered with dozens of pictures (mostly of flowers and kittens) and ghastly plaques saying things like *You don't have to be pretty to be a Fairy, but it helps.* There was a big calendar pinned up as well. It was decorated with butterflies. Friday the thirteenth – Awakening Day – was ringed in pink.

But it was the Fairies I was really interested in. They weren't what I was expecting at all. In fact, I got quite a shock when I saw them.

They were *old*. They still wore the same sort of draughty, pastel-coloured net frocks, but they were topped up with a million layers of lumpy jumpers, woolly cardigans, shawls, wraps and mufflers. You couldn't see their wings at all.

I stared at them, trying to match them up with their younger versions. One or two had really shrunk. Others, quite frankly, looked like they'd had one pudding too many over the last hundred and sixteen years.

Some wore wigs like stiff versions of their youthful hair-dos. Some had gone in for blue-rinsed perms. A few wore hairnets. Still others had their grey locks pulled back into buns. Three wore spectacles, and several had hearing-aids. Nobody seemed to bothering with a Wand any more, I noticed. Instead, they all had big, stern, navy-blue handbags placed carefully within reach.

They were variously occupied. Blue and Yellow were knitting. Lilac was crocheting what looked like a baby's bonnet. Green and Lavender were flicking through the latest issues of *Fairy World* and *Hi!*. Apricot was eating a banana. Silver, White and Peach were dozing with their mouths open. Gold was doing a puzzle. Tangerine and Pink were playing Scrabble.

'Please,' I announced humbly to the room. 'Please'ms, Oi've come to get the dirties.' And I did the usual bob.

Nobody even looked my way. They just tucked their feet in and moved their handbags closer to give me a bit of room, then carried on with what they were doing. All except Apricot, who chucked her banana skin on a nearby coffee table and said vaguely:

'There's a good girl.'

I left my trolley parked by the door and began wandering around collecting up cereal bowls, jam pots, dirty coffee cups and plates of cold toast crusts.

'What time is it?' enquired Yellow suddenly, looking up from her knitting.

Everyone, including me, looked at the tall pink and gold grandfather clock which stood in a corner. It was one minute to nine.

'Nearly time,' said Blue, sounding excited. 'One minute to go.'

'Oooh!' squealed Lilac, putting down her crochet hook and reaching for her handbag. 'Wait. I need my glasses.'

Their voices had changed too. They were no longer high and silvery. They sounded old and quavery, like cracked bells.

There was an air of expectancy in the room. Scrabble, knitting, magazines and puzzles were cast aside. Cushions were plumped up. They were all getting themselves ready for some sort of treat, that was clear. What, though?

Gold took a packet of mints from her bag, popped one in her mouth and said:

'Go on, Rose. You do the honours.'

'Shall I?' said Rose, the Pink Fairy.

'Yes, yes, go on, dear,' came a clamour of voices. For some reason, everyone was staring eagerly at the blank wall.

'You don't think it's too early?'

'No, no, dear, it's on the dot. Do it now!'

'All right then,' said Rose. 'Who's got the remote?'

'Who knows? You had it last, Ivy.'

The remote turned out to be a small, black, oblong object. The Green Fairy (Ivy) finally located it down the side of the sofa and handed it ceremoniously to Rose, who pointed it at the blank wall. As she did so, the pink velvet curtains drew themselves together of their own accord, shutting out the daylight. I paused, hands full of dishes. I couldn't see a thing in the gloom.

Much to my surprise, the blank wall kind of wobbled. There was a rippling effect before it steadied and I found myself looking into a turret room. It was plainly furnished in a masculine, no-nonsense sort of way. Brass bed, oak wardrobe, table with a china jug and washbowl and shaving mirror. A sheathed sword hung on a belt from a hook behind the door. A bow and sheaf of arrows were propped in one corner. A punch bag was set up in another.

In the middle of the room, a large young man dressed only in breeches and vest was struggling to raise a heavily weighted bar. He had got it to chest height and was obviously aiming even higher. He was very good-looking, if you like that sort of thing. Blond, shoulder-length hair, lantern jaw, good nose, decent teeth. Tall. Muscular. Healthy outdoor type. Scarlettine would have liked him.

So did the Fairies. They were twittering and cooing among themselves, like pigeons.

'*Lovely* young man. So strong.'

'Looks like he washed his hair again last night.'

'She *will* like him, won't she? Beauty.'

'Oh, goes without saying. They'll make a lovely couple.'

'A very good choice on our part.'

So. This must be Prince Brett. We were watching him on what had been referred to in the kitchen as the Magic Screen. I had to admit it was excellent. Perfect picture, not a sign of interference. Good sound quality too. You could hear Prince Brett huffing and puffing as he strained to lift the bar. Suddenly he got his weight beneath it and lifted it high above his head, arms straight, though quivering slightly.

'Hooray!' cheered the Fairies. Clapping broke out.

Thump! The Prince staggered and dropped the bar with a gasp of relief. He strolled to the centre of the screen and faced his watching audience full on. He flexed his muscles a couple of times, bared his dashing white teeth in a smile, then adopted the sort of hand-on-hip, heroic pose that you would only try out if you thought you were alone and unobserved. I had a feeling he was looking at himself in a full-length mirror. He had no idea that he was being spied on. I couldn't help feeling a bit sorry for him. It comes to something when you can't even do a bit of private posing without being observed by a room full of old Fairies.

'Sit-ups next,' observed Blue knowingly. 'You watch.'

'Oh, I don't think so, Iris, dear,' said Yellow. 'It's push-ups. He always does push-ups after the weights. Doesn't he, Lilac?'

'Running on the spot, I thought,' observed Lilac. 'Although you may be right, Primrose. Sometimes he does the push-ups before the running.'

'But he always ends with the punch bag,' nodded Gold. There was general agreement.

'Oh, yes. Marigold's right. He always ends with the punch bag.'

'*Lovely* young man.'

'Oh, yes. *Lovely.*'

They even knew the poor chap's exercise routine! They must do this every morning.

Prince Brett began running on the spot.

'You see?' said Lilac, nudging Primrose. 'I said it was the running next, dear.'

Very quietly, I tiptoed over to the trolley and deposited the dirty dishes. I didn't want to draw attention to myself – although I needn't have worried. All twelve Fairies were glued to the Screen. Watching Prince Brett do his morning work-out was far more interesting than watching a humble kitchen maid collect dishes.

'I suppose we should check on the palace,' said Apricot, who was eating another banana. 'Turn it over, Rose.'

'In a minute,' said Rose. 'Let's just see this bit.'

Prince Brett had finished running on the spot and was now doing sideways lunges.

'Oooh,' said Silver. 'That's new. Haven't seen him doing those before.'

'I still think we should check on Beauty,' insisted Apricot. 'And we should look at the crossroads where we're putting the signpost. There could be road works or something, you never know. Go on, Rose, dear. Just a quick check, to set our minds at ease.'

Rose pointed the remote again – and the scene changed. We were now looking into a dark attic room. I recognized it immediately. Beauty lay stretched out in the pile of flax, exactly as she had fallen one hundred years before. There was a little smile on her lips. She looked as though she was dreaming pleasant dreams.

'Ahhhh,' sighed the Fairies. 'Sleeping like a baby. Bless. Keep going, Rose.'

The scene changed again. This time, we were in a forest, at a place where three roads met. Well, tracks, really. They certainly didn't look like they were used much. The forest was dark and choked with undergrowth. There seemed very little space between the trees.

'Two o'clock tomorrow afternoon,' remarked Silver. 'That's when we have to get him there. I can't wait to see his face when the Enchanted Path appears. An hour should be plenty of time, don't you think?'

'More than enough, Silvia,' agreed Tangerine. 'Muscles like that, won't take him long to hack through. Twenty minutes along the Path, ten minutes to deal with the brambles, and another half an hour to find his way through the palace and up to the attic. And at three o'clock …'

'The Kiss!' twittered the assembled company. 'Ooooh! The Kiss!'

'Just think. Three o'clock tomorrow, we'll be watching it live!'

'Then we break open the champagne!'

'And put on the party hats!'

'And blow squeakers and pull crackers …'

'And set the bells ringing all over the land!'

'And dance! Don't forget the dancing! You did remember to book the band, Lily?'

'Of course I did, dear. What do you take me for?'

'And the feast!' chimed in Lavender (one of the plump ones). 'Don't forget the feast!'

Just then, I fouled up. I admit it. I leaned against the trolley, which was fatally overloaded, causing a landslide of dirty crocks to come crashing to the floor.

Instantly, the forest scene vanished and was replaced with the blank wall. Twelve faces were staring at me accusingly.

'Sorry, missuses, Oi didn't mean to, please, sorry,' I gibbered, bobbing up and down like a yoyo.

'You're new, aren't you?' enquired Peach, quite kindly.

'Yes'm.'

'What's your name?'

'Eliza, mum, please'm, sorry.'

'Well, Eliza, you're trying to get too much on to the trolley, dear. I should take what you've got and come back for the rest. Better still, send one of the leprechauns. There's a skill in loading a trolley.'

'Oi will, mum, Oi will. Oi'll just pick up these broken dishes …'

'Leave it, dear. There are things we need to talk about. Off you go, there's a good girl.'

So off I went, trundling the trolley before me. The pink door shut firmly behind me, I retraced my steps up the corridor. The trolley kept bashing into the walls. Yet more crockery crashed to the floor. The kitchen door flew open.

'What eez going on?' screamed Chef Basin, waving his arms. 'What eez zees yeu do, stupeeed girl! What a mess yeu make! Where 'ave yeu been?'

'Please, sir, collectin' the plates loike what you told me, sir …'

'*Smashing* ze plates, more like! Mary, take over 'ere, ze girl ees an 'ow-you-say *eembecile. Yeu!*' He pointed grimly. 'Get over to ze sink. *Jump to eet!*'

So I went over to the sink, which by now was piled high with a veritable mountain of yucky pots, pans and greasy plates, rolled up my sleeves and got stuck in.

Still. I had found out what I needed to know. That was some consolation.

14. BACK TO STARKACRE

Ten long, long hours later, at sunset, when the siren blared and all the leprechauns downed spoons and began taking off their aprons, I picked up a big bucket of potato peelings and casually made my way to the door.

'What ye doin', darlin'?' asked Shaun. ''Tis knock-off time.'

'Please, sir, takin' the peelin's to the dustbins loike Chef asked, sir.'

'He did? Aye, well, fair enough. Hurry along in and Mary'll get ye some broth.'

I dropped a bob and hurried out. I dumped the bucket next to the bins, tore off my filthy, wet apron and slipped through the gate. Nobody saw me leave.

I ran around to the front and sprinted across the field. The sky was pink. The sun's last rays were about to disappear below the distant trees.

The blackened Faerie Ring was still there, on the edge of the wood. Ralph was lying down next to it, snoozing. Some guard wolf. He leaped to his feet as I came hurrying up, making out he'd been wide awake all along.

'Where are the lambs?' I enquired.

'What lambsh?' asked Ralph.

'There were lambs. Gambolling ones. Three of them. Where are they?'

'Oh, *thoshe* lambsh. A shepherd came and took them away,' said Ralph. He eyed me shiftily, yawned and pretended to scratch at a flea. I didn't know whether to believe him or not.

Surely he wouldn't? Not in Fairyland?

'*You* look a mesh,' he observed disapprovingly. 'Shmall girlsh are shupposhed to look neat and clean. And tender.'

Tender? What did he mean by that? Kind to little bunny rabbits sort of tender? Or tender as in roast beef?

'I'm not small. I'm twelve,' I reminded him sharply. 'And I'm the youngest daughter from a long line of wicked queens. We don't do neat. Anyway, shut up. I've spent the last two days washing up with a load of noisy leprechauns and a mad chef. I don't want to talk. Are we going or what?'

'Yeah, yeah. Get in the Ring, then.'

I stepped into it. Ralph loped in and stood beside me. Then he lifted his head and Howled, with a capital H. It was a spine-chilling Howl that didn't belong in Fairyland at all. It did the trick, though.

A split second later, we were back in Great-Aunt Angry's dark room. She was still sitting in her armchair. The fire had gone out. I wondered if she had been to bed since we left.

'There ye are!' she cried. 'How did it go? What did ye discover? Come on, out with it!'

I didn't reply for a moment. I was too busy choking on the green smoke. The pale green circle was already fading away. Tail wagging, Ralph padded over and gave her hand a lick of greeting. She smacked him on the nose and he retired to the hearth, looking hurt.

'Come on!' shouted my great-auntie again, waving her Stick. 'Did ye see 'em, the Fairies?'

'Yes, yes, I saw them.'

'Well, go on, then. What are they like these days? Still smug, I'll bet.'

'Well – no. Actually, they've changed quite a lot.'

'Changed? How changed?'

'Well – they're old. Just a lot of dear old biddies with cardigans and hairnets.'

'Oh?' Aunt Angry reflected on this. 'Let themselves go at last, then. Well, 'tis hard work, keepin' yerself young for eternity. I never bothered. Looks ain't everythin'. Sooner conserve me Power for important things. Must say I'm surprised, though. Thought they were too vain.'

'Well, they're not any more. Actually, they seemed rather sweet.'

'*Sweet!*' scoffed my great-auntie. Her hair flew around a bit. She spat on the floor. 'Hear that, Ralph? Sweet, she calls 'em. Just shows how much she knows. What did ye find out? Hurry up, I got to make me plans.'

So I told her. I told her all about the Magic Screen and Prince Brett and the crossroads in the forest. I told her about the planned signpost and the Enchanted Path. And about the timing, of course, which was crucial. She took it all in, nodding darkly.

'... and then he kisses her, on the dot of three,' I finished. 'And she wakes, as young and lovely as before. I saw her, actually, on the Magic Screen. She does look exactly the same.'

'Right. I think I got that. So they got one o' them fancy Magic Screens. I nearly got one meself, but the salesman got on me nerves. Better than my Pool, is it?'

'Oh no. Well, it's bigger. But the reception's about the same.'

'Aye. I'll have to swot up on that. Different sort of transmission. Still, shouldn't be too hard. I got the brochure somewhere. The Prince reaches the crossroads at two o'clock, ye say?'

'Yep.'

'Right. So that's when we gets him. Ye done good, Wilma. How did it go, by the way? Did you get on all right? They didn't suspect nothin', I 'ope?'

'I spent two days washing up and eating leprechaun broth. By the way, guess who was the cook? Your Chef Basin.'

'Really?' Her eyebrows shot up. 'So that's what

'appened to 'im. Well, well. There's a come-down in the world. Still mad, I s'pose? Well, must be, cookin' for a bunch of old Fairies.'

'Yep. Er — what did you mean, *get* him? The Prince? How exactly?'

'We cunningly lures him away.'

'Lure him away? How do we do that? The Fairies will be watching the whole thing on the Screen. They'll be cheering him on every bit of the way.'

'Aye. And that's when I'll be setting up a spot of Magical Interference.'

'A spot of what?'

'You know. When the picture goes funny. Wiggly lines. Then it goes blank.'

'How do you propose to do that?'

'With me Power, 'o course. I'll scramble the signal.'

'You can do that?'

''Course I can. Not for long, mind. It takes a bit o' doin'. I'll be harnessin' lightnin' an' callin' up winds and splittin' molecules and all sorts while doin' difficult calculations in me head at the same time. So ye'll have to be quick.'

'*I'll* have to be quick? Quick doing what?'

'Quick with the lurin'. Lurin' the Prince into the Ring.'

'What Ring?' I was really confused.

'The Faerie Ring, what else? Look, it's quite simple. I sends you along in the Ring and you lures him into it. Soon as he's in, Ralph'll give the signal and I'll get ye all back here, pronto.'

'I see. And how am I supposed to lure him into the

Ring? He's six foot two and built like a wardrobe. Do I *wrestle* him in?'

''Course not. He's got to enter it voluntarily. That's the Law.'

'Then how?'

'Ye'll 'ave to use yer feminine wiles. The old maiden in distress scam. He's a Prince, ain't he? They always falls for that one.'

'What sort of distress?'

'Well, let me see. He's a strong lad, ye say?'

'Yes. So?'

'So say ye needs a piano shiftin'.'

'Right. A piano.' Actually, it was quite a good idea. I had the feeling that Prince Brett would see shifting a piano on his own as a challenge.

'That's it. Nothin' to it. Soon as he's in the Ring, I'll take over. Once he's over the threshold, he's mine. I win. No Prince, no Kiss. Beauty'll sleep on. And there's nothin' they can do about it.'

'Er –' I said.

'Er what? What now?'

'What will happen to him?' I enquired. 'You won't put him in that room, will you? The one with all the – others?'

'Why?' She stared up at me. Her hair was beginning to stir. 'What do you care? Are ye with me or not? Is there one member of this family I can count on?'

'I'm with you,' I sighed. 'Don't worry, you can count on me, Aunt Angry.'

I don't know why I called her that. It just slipped out.

'What did you just call me?' she asked, after a little pause.

'Aunt Angry. Great-Aunt Angria's a bit of a mouthful, isn't it? Why? Don't you like it?'

There was another little pause. Then she said:

'Ain't been called that in a long time. Grimelza always called me that, when we was kids. She was Grim an' I was Angry.'

'Not surprising you didn't get on, then,' I remarked.

'Eh?'

'Nothing. Would you rather I didn't call you it?'

'No. That's all right. Ye can call me it, I s'pose. But only when it's us. Not in front of people, right?'

'Right.'

'Good. That's sorted, then. So. Goin' back to what we was sayin'. Ye're sure ye're with me? I don't need no backsliders.'

'Yes. I've already said. I'm with you.'

But I wasn't really happy about it.

A short time later, totally exhausted after two days' hard graft, I sat in bed. Well, on bed was more like it. I didn't have a sheet, remember? There was nothing to get into, unless I lay on the springs underneath the mattress.

Tired though I was, I did my guitar practice. I played the chord of C at least three times. I think it was C. It sounded a bit funny. Oh no! I had gone backwards! I made a mental note to check the fingering with Alvis, next time I saw him.

Then I decided to give Mother a quick call. I thought she would appreciate it, with all she was going through. I would be a calming influence.

For once, I got her first time.

'Yes?' she said tiredly. 'What is it, Wilma?'

She was in the Coach. Good. Things couldn't be that bad, then.

'I just wanted to catch up,' I explained. 'On the family news. By the way, I've just spent two days washing up in Fairyland.'

'Lovely. Look, darling, I don't want to rush you, but I have to get off the Ball. Things are quite, quite critical. We've had another postcard from Scarlettine. She's thinking of marrying the pirate chief! His name is Jack the Kipper. Or maybe Jack the Skipper, I couldn't quite make out the writing. Whichever it is, he sounds fishy and I don't like the sound of him. Oh, if only she'd taken her *Ball*! And Frostia's work-force have walked off the site again. And Alvis hasn't come back, and Daddy's getting frantic about the mulch. And poor Maud doesn't know what to do about Grandma. She's refusing to come home, although Maud and Frank think that the other gypsies feel she's outstayed her welcome. And all that camp-fire food is upsetting her system. Beans and so forth. And it's such a *little* caravan. Although I *did* say. "Mama can be difficult, Maud," I said. "Are you quite sure about this?"'

'The hundred-year spell is up tomorrow,' I said. 'My job is to help Aunt Angry muck it up. Innocent people are involved. What should I do, do you think?'

'Don't interrupt, darling. I was about to tell you about Uncle Bacchus. *Search parties are out!*'

Gosh. Search parties, eh?

'It's serious, then,' I said.

'Yes. And Denzil hasn't returned. Mrs Pudding has got

125

the kitchen staff out beating the grounds. We've got nothing to eat. I haven't got time to organize it. We're living on Daddy's tomatoes. Not the ones for the show, of course. Darling, I *must* go. I've got the world on my shoulders.'

'That's nothing,' I said gloomily. 'You think you've got problems? You should try living here.'

15. BREAKFAST WITH AUNT ANGRY

'So how are things at 'ome?'

It was the following morning – Friday the thirteenth, BAD. (That stands for Beauty's Awakening Day, of course. Thought of that myself. Clever, eh?) I was sitting at the table in the squalid kitchen, eating my horrible porridge. I'd had a good night's sleep for once. No dreams, no ghosts. Aunt Angry must have had a word.

I had company this morning. Aunt Angry was sitting on a chair opposite, with a mug of tea. She had her shoes on today. Her swollen feet were definitely going down. Mother's gout cream really seemed to be doing the trick.

'Pardon?' I said.

'You heard. I knows ye been talkin' to yer ma on the Ball at night.'

'How do you know?'

'I got my ways. I knows more than ye think. I hears ye practisin' yer guitar too.'

'Really?' At last, someone was showing an interest. 'What do you think?'

'Don't give up yer day job. So. Everythin' all right, is it? At 'ome?'

'No, actually,' I said. 'There are a few problems.'

'Such as? Might as well tell me while I'm drinkin' me tea.'

So I told her everything. All about Grandma's new, exotic gypsy life-style and Frostia's problems with the cowboy Inuits and Daddy's mulch crisis and Alvis's continued absence and Scarlettine's engagement to a kipper and the mystery of my missing Uncle Bacchus. The only thing I didn't mention was Denzil. I was so worried I couldn't even bring myself to talk about him, particularly as I had the feeling that Aunt Angry wouldn't care twopence. I had hoped he might come thumping on to my bed in the night, but he hadn't.

She listened to it all, sipping her tea and staring at me with her hooded eyes.

'So Grimelza's finally flipped,' she said, with some satisfaction, when I finally chugged to a halt. ''Twas only a matter of time. Coupla thousand years, that's all it took.'

'Well, I wouldn't say *flipped*,' I said, feeling I should defend Grandma, whom I'm very fond of, despite everything. 'She's just enjoying herself. Letting her hair down. They should let her get on with it and stop fussing so much.'

'Hmm. No hair left to let down, by the look of her. By the way, yer ma should use a Scrying Glass.'

'What?'

'If she wants to talk to your sister Scarlettine an' find out where Bacchus has got to. Might raise yer cousin Alvis too. Scrying Glasses might be old-fashioned these days, but they're a darned sight more reliable than Crystal Balls.'

'Do you know, that's not a bad idea,' I said. 'I'll mention that when I see her. I'm sure we must have an old one somewhere. Up in the attic, I'll bet.'

Just then, Ralph came slinking through the wolf flap. I should mention that, although it wasn't yet nine o'clock, we'd already had a run-in. He had been sitting at the bottom of the stairs when I came down from my room. I was just about to walk past, when, right out of the blue, he demanded to know whether I thought he had big teeth! I told him, in no uncertain terms, that the only big thing about him was his mouth, and he had stalked off with his nose in the air.

He stopped short and eyed us both.

'What's up with you?' asked Aunt Angry.

'Nothing,' said Ralph sulkily. And loped off without another glance.

'What *is* it with him?' I asked, as soon as he had gone.

'How d'ye mean?'

'Well, he's a bit *odd,* don't you think? He keeps coming out with all this weird stuff about red cloaks and cottages and flowers and little baskets with pink cakes in. And asking me whether I think bits of him are big.'

'Yeah, well, it runs in his family, don't it? One of his ancestors was what you might call notorious. Don't ye know the story?'

'No,' I said. 'What story?'

Aunt Angry told me. It took a while. It was quite good, actually, if a bit unbelievable. My porridge got cold while I listened.

'... and out stepped granny, alive an' well!' she finished triumphantly, and took another slurp of her tea.

'That's ridiculous,' I scoffed. 'As if a wolf could eat a full-size old woman in one gulp, without chewing. She'd never go down. And even if she did, I'm sure she wouldn't feel *well*. Not after being in a wolf's stomach. It stands to reason.'

'Aye. Anyway, that's how the story goes. The important thing is, Ralph believes it.'

'So he thinks he's a what – reincarnation or something? Of this unlikely ancestor of his who's supposed to have swallowed Little Red Whatsit's granny?'

'Not exactly a reincarnation. He's more sort of following in the footsteps, if ye get my meanin'. Goin' back to 'is roots. I suppose it makes 'im feel important. Well, he don't have much of a life, here with me. I ain't the most patient of employers. Specially when me feet are givin' me gyp.'

'How are they this morning?' I enquired. 'Better?'

'Aye. I must say that cream of yer ma's is good stuff. Anyway, about Ralph. Don't say I said anythin'. I wouldn't want 'im to think I was talkin' about 'im

behind 'is back. I tell ye somethin', though ...' She gave
a little chuckle.

'What?'

''E dresses up sometimes. In an old frilly mob cap he
found, an' a pair o' my old glasses. He don't think I
knows, but I do.'

I laughed out loud. I just couldn't help it. Although,
actually, it was a bit sad.

There was something else on my mind. I thought I
might as well mention it now, seeing we were getting on
so well.

'Aunt Angry?' I said.

'What?'

'About that room. The one along the passage. Where
you keep those − people.'

'The Room o' Livin' Statues? What about it?'

'What did they do that was so bad?'

'This an' that. Cheeky, mainly. Not showin' me
respect. One or two tried to cheat me. Flippin' goat ate
me cardi. Milkmaid short-changed me. Pig looked at me
funny. Cats dug up me bulbs. Why?'

'Don't you think it's a bit harsh?'

'Harsh? 'Course it's harsh. They don't call me the
Thirteenth Faerie for nothin', girl. Cross me, an' that's
what they gets. Anyway,' she downed the last of her cold
tea, 'this won't do. Got to go an' make me final
preparations.'

'Can I watch?' I asked.

'Certainly not.'

'But I'm on work experience. I'm supposed to be
learning things.'

131

'Ye *are* learnin' things. 'Ow to do as ye're told, for one. Ye're here to do the donkey work, girl. I does the clever stuff. How far have ye got with yer Magic Exams?'

'Grade Three. I've got my certificate upstairs, if you want to see it. I'm taking Four soon.'

'There ye are then. What I'm about to do is degree level, way beyond you. This is the Big One, Wilma. The one that'll put me back on top, where I belongs. I been waitin' for this day for a hundred years. Got to concentrate. Can't afford to get it wrong. Anyway, I likes to work on me own. That's the way I've always done things. On me own.'

'Oh,' I said, disappointed. I really wanted to see Aunt Angry preparing for the Big One, as she called it. Scrambling a Magic signal is virtually impossible. It takes immense Power. I'd read that in one of Mother's Advanced Magick books.

'So I'll see ye down in the lab just before two. 'Tis almost ten o'clock now. Ralph'll come and get ye when 'tis time. Till then, I don't want to be disturbed, right?'

'Right.'

Then she vanished. No bothering with a Magic Ring, no puff of smoke, no fiddling with the knob of her Stick, nothing.

It's very hard to do that. I was impressed. She certainly hadn't lost her touch.

I had four long hours ahead of me. What was I to do?

I'll tell you what I did. I looked for Denzil. I wandered through cold, silent passages, and up and down flights of stairs, calling his name. I looked behind ragged curtains and under chairs and tables. I pulled open cupboard doors. I tried doorknobs, some of which turned and some which didn't. I explored empty, cobwebby rooms where the furniture was draped spookily in dust sheets. I tried the organ room. There was no sign of either the phantom organist or Denzil, so I came out again. I looked at the door next to it. The one behind which all those enchanted ones stood around in darkness, frozen in the grip of the Magical force field.

I didn't go in there. I just couldn't.

Anyway, despite all my efforts, there was no sign of the wretched animal. Finally, I gave up. I went back up to my attic room and looked in my trusty trunk, deciding what I needed for the day ahead. There was nothing to eat, sadly. My Grade Three Certificate would only be a nuisance. So would the guitar. I couldn't see a lot of point in taking a punctured hot-water bottle, or Graham, for that matter, who was shedding stuffing like nobody's business. I didn't think I'd have any need for Magic Candles.

I just took my Wand and my MoBall. I slipped them into the pocket of my cloak and lay on the bed, watching dark, ominous clouds gather through the tiny window. It looked like another storm was brewing, wouldn't you know. I suppose I could have done my guitar practice, but somehow I didn't feel in a musical mood. I didn't have a watch, so I had no idea of the time.

I dozed off, more out of boredom than tiredness. Some time later, a scratching on the door awoke me with a jolt. I scrambled off the bed and went to open it. Ralph was outside. I stood waiting for some daft remark about baskets or flowers or some such nonsense, but for once he didn't mention them.

'It ish time,' he growled briefly. 'Follow me.'

In silence, I followed his bushy tail back down to the dungeons.

Aunt Angry was seated at her workbench in her tip of a lab. She had placed a square of clean white cloth over the charred surface. On it was a collection of weird objects. Ancient weighing scales, filled with feathers. A gyroscope. A twisted piece of metal that I recognized as a lightning conductor. A tall jar filled with thick green liquid, which was bubbling and glopping all on its own. Her Scrying Glass. A thick, leather-bound book with pieces of paper sticking out, marking the important pages.

She was wearing her pointy hat again. She had new shoes on, too. Black patent, with a heel. I suspected she'd been saving them for this very moment.

'Ready?' she said. 'I've done the Ring.'

She had, too. A perfect green circle glowed gently amid all the clutter on the floor.

'What are you doing?' I asked curiously. 'What's all that stuff?'

'Never you mind. Ye'll learn all about it when ye're ready, and that ain't yet. Come on, get in the Ring. You too, Ralph.'

'Does he have to come?' I said. Ralph lifted a lip and sneered.

''Course. He's got to give the Howl, ain't ye, Ralph? In ye get, the pair o' you.'

Reluctantly, I followed Ralph into the Ring. I admit I was beginning to feel quite nervous. It was a big responsibility, luring Prince Brett, and I wasn't sure I was up to it.

'Right,' said Aunt Angry. 'Now, let's run over it one last time. I'll set ye down just before the crossroads. He comes ridin' along. Ye asks him to shift a piano. Ye lures him into the Ring.'

'Supposing – just *supposing* something goes wrong?' I enquired. 'With the luring, I mean? I've never lured before.'

'It had better not,' snapped Aunt Angry, shooting me a hard stare. 'Ye can't expect any help from me. I'll be too busy scramblin' the signal so them twelve do-gooders can't see what's happenin'. Like I said, I can't do it for long, so don't 'ang about. Five minutes is all ye got. Want to synchronize watches?'

'I don't have a w—'

'Never mind, never mind, just be as quick as ye can. It's one minute to two. Go! Now!'

And she twisted the silver knob on her Stick. There was the usual bang, flash, and puff of green smoke – and off I went a-luring!

16. LURING

There we were, Ralph and I, standing in the familiar circle of blackened grass. We were in a forest which was nothing like the pretty, manicured Fairy wood. This was a proper forest – dark, ancient and, frankly, quite daunting. The trees were gnarled, twisted things, covered with moss. There were a lot of brambles and pot holes. There were no flowers, butterflies or babbling streams. No birds sang here. Our Faerie Ring blended in quite nicely.

I recognized where I was immediately. Through the trees, a short way off, I saw the crossroads where the three roads met. I had seen this place before, on the Magic Screen in the Fairies' lounge. This time, though, there were a couple of differences.

There was an old, worm-eaten signpost standing at the crossroads which hadn't been there before. On it were the carved words: *To the Enchanted Palace*. It pointed to a fourth road that also hadn't been there the last time. It was a twisting silver pathway, carving its way through the undergrowth and leading off into the distance. It looked as though it was made of moonlight, although it was early afternoon. A Magical haze lay above it, rather like ground mist, but more romantic. Star shine, perhaps. It seemed to shimmer and there was a greasy smell to it.

That was when I heard the sound of hoofs, coming closer at a fast trot.

'It's him!' I hissed. 'Prince Brett! He's coming! What shall I do?'

'Waylay him, of courshe,' snapped Ralph. 'Go on. You're doing the luring. I'm shtaying here to –'

'– guard the Ring. Yeah, yeah,' I finished tiredly. 'How come it's always me?'

And I stepped out of the Ring and hurried through the trees to the road, just as the Prince came riding around the bend.

He was looking rather splendid, actually. He wore a green tunic over a white, frilly shirt, matching green tights, and a short riding cape. His muscular legs were encased in long leather riding boots with spurs on. A feathered cap sat jauntily on his head. A sword hung at his belt. Today, his long hair was caught back in a pony tail. As a rule, I dislike men with pony tails – but I had to admit it suited him.

I stepped into the road and flagged him down. He hauled on the reins and came to a halt. The horse snorted crossly. It was black and shiny, rather like Clint and Horace, although it couldn't fly, of course.

'Yes?' said Prince Brett, frowning slightly.

It seemed a bit abrupt. There was no 'Good morrow, fair maiden, how may I help thee?' or anything of that nature. Just 'Yes?' Short, clipped, and rather impatient. He obviously just saw me as a small, annoying girl who was about to ruin his morning ride. Which I was, I suppose.

There was no point in beating about the bush. I decided to cut to the chase.

'Hello,' I said. 'I've got a piano needs shifting. I wonder, would you mind?'

There was a little pause. Then:

'What sort of piano?' he said, staring down at me, brow still furrowed.

'A big one. Very heavy. It's in my gran's cottage, back there.' I waved my arm in the direction of the way I had come. 'She wants it up in her bedroom. It looks daft in the kitchen.'

Prince Brett was still staring. He put his head on one side and said suspiciously:

'You're not a witch in disguise, by any chance? Come to lead me off my chosen course?'

'Who, *me*? A *witch*? Of course not. Ha, ha, ha, the very thought,' I laughed merrily. There's no doubt about it. I should go on the stage.

'Ha, ha, ha!' To my relief, Prince Brett's brow cleared and he joined in my merriment. 'No, I suppose not. Sorry, little girl. Just checking.'

'Yes. Look, about the piano. We can't do it on our own, me and Gran, we're not strong enough.'

Prince Brett tossed back his head and gave another short laugh.

'Ha, ha, ha! No,' he said, highly amused. 'No, you wouldn't be. Takes a man to do a job like that. Good thing I came along, eh? All right, young miss, you've convinced me. I'll come and ...' His voice trailed off. He was looking past my shoulder, up ahead to the crossroads where the signpost stood and the quivering silver road led away to who knows where. *Blast!*

'What's up?' I asked, all innocence.

'Am I seeing things? Does that road look silver to you?'

'Ground mist,' I said promptly. 'We get it a lot round here. So what about this piano?'

'One moment. There appears to be a new signpost. I must have ridden this way a dozen times and I don't recall any signpost. I can't quite make out what it says. And I thought there were only three roads.'

'They've been doing some forest-improvement work,' I told him. 'Gran's furious, says the hammering's keeping her awake at night. They're building a new road to the dump. That's what the signpost says. *To the Dump.* Look, about this piano. If you think it's too heavy for you, just say so. We'll ask someone else.'

'No, no,' said Prince Brett hastily. I could see he was hurt by the implied criticism. 'Just the one piano, is it?'

'Just the one.'

'No problem. Leave it to me. All in a day's work.' He jumped down off his horse, looped the bridle over a branch and spat on his hands. 'Lead on, little girl. Take me to this piano of yours.'

139

I led him into the trees. He seemed quite keen, actually. He was limbering up, dancing on his toes and punching the air, looking forward to pitting his strength against the weight of an imaginary piano. He was even whistling.

All of that stopped when he saw Ralph.

He grabbed my arm with one hand and drew his sword with the other.

'Get back!' he hissed, pushing me behind him in a heroic sort of way.

'Why?' I said innocently. 'What's up?'

'*Wolf!* Right ahead, by that patch of blackened grass. Don't you see? Stay there. Leave this to me.'

'That's not a wolf,' I told him. 'That's Woofy, our doggy. He wouldn't hurt a fly. Would you, Woofy?' Honestly. How I think of it all.

Ralph eyed me nastily. He didn't say anything, but I could see he wasn't keen on being Woofy the doggy.

'Come on, Woofy!' I cried, rubbing it in. 'There's a good dog. Ready for a nice bone, Woofy? Good old Woofles. Good old Woofy boy.'

I pushed past Prince Brett, marched up to Ralph and ruffled him hard on his head. I pulled his ear in an affectionate way. I would have kissed him on the nose, but saw the look in his eyes and decided not to push my luck.

'See?' I said to the Prince, who was staring on in amazement. 'Completely harmless. An old softy, aren't you, Woofy? Give the gentleman a paw, there's a good boy.'

Looking sick, Ralph raised an unwilling paw and let

it hang in the air. On any real dog, this would be appealing. Somehow, though, it didn't go with his slavering jaws and the low, threatening growl issuing from his throat.

It convinced Prince Brett, though.

'Well, blow me down,' he said, ruefully scratching his head beneath his feathered hat. 'I could have sworn it was a wolf.'

'Come and shake his paw, then,' I said. 'He can't keep it dangling there all day, can you, Woofy? Old Woofy dog?'

'Right. Yes of course,' said Prince Brett, sheathing his sword and advancing towards the Ring with outstretched hand. 'Hello there, Woofy, you're a very fine fellow, aren't you?' He stepped into the Ring. 'I've got dogs of my own back home, but I must say none of them looks like –'

'*Ooooooooooooowwwwwwwwwwwwwwwwwwww!*'

Prince Brett snatched his hand back as Ralph threw back his head and let out a hair-raising Howl that rang through the treetops. Any traces of reluctant Woofyness had gone. Now he was All Wolf.

'What the –?'

Bang! White flash. Puff of green smoke. And we were back at Starkacre.

The Ring landed us in the main hall. Outside, surprise, surprise, a storm was raging. Thunder cracked, winds howled, lightning flickered through the high windows, adding extra drama to the scene within. Not that it needed more drama. It was pretty spectacular enough already.

Aunt Angry was standing dead centre, on the dais that held the timer, the clock and the old spinning-wheel – which blazed with green light, as though it was on fire. She seemed taller, somehow – but maybe that was because she was wearing her pointy hat and heels. Her hair lashed and whipped around her in a frenzy. She held her Stick in her left hand, straight above her head. I could see her arm shaking with the effort. Green sparks were crackling up and down its length. I felt the Power coming off her in waves. The veins were standing out on her forehead.

At this moment in time, I didn't think of her as my great-auntie. At this moment, she was the Thirteenth Faerie.

Her eyes had rolled back in her head. You could only see the whites.

'Auntie!' I shouted. I feared for her, I really did. 'You can stop now! We're back! We've got him!'

Suddenly, she staggered. She put out her hand to steady herself. If the spinning-wheel hadn't been there, I think she would have fallen. Her eyes returned to normal, and slowly she lowered her Stick. The green sparks fizzed away to nothing. Her hair subsided and hung limply down her back. The spinning-wheel lost its green fire and became just an old, cobwebby piece of junk.

'Phew!' she said, wiping her brow. 'That was close. Don't think I could 'ave held it for much longer.'

I moved forward to help her down, but she held up one hand and I stopped. She was staring at Prince Brett, who was still standing in the Ring, his face a mask of dazed bewilderment. He was gazing around, probably looking for the piano. He didn't even have the wherewithal to draw his sword. I felt quite sorry for him.

'So ye're the one they chose,' she said. 'Nice muscles. Shame about the spell.'

'Spell?' said Prince Brett faintly. 'What spell?'

'This spell,' said my wicked auntie. And she pointed her Stick at him.

He must have guessed something horrible was about to happen, because he automatically flung up his arm to shield his face. It didn't do him any good, though.

There was another flash of green light – and he froze. That's the only way I can describe it. One second, he was a living, breathing, handsome young man. The next, he was a statue – stiff, still, utterly impassive. It was as if the life force had been sucked out of him, leaving an empty shell.

Rather shakily, Great-Aunt Angria climbed down from the dais, grimacing as her poor old feet made contact with the floor. Her new shoes were pinching, I could tell. Ralph padded across and licked her hand. Vaguely, she patted his head.

'I'm all right,' she said. 'Took it out of me a bit, but I'm all right.'

Then she hobbled up to Prince Brett, stared him up and down and snapped her fingers before his nose. His unseeing eyes gazed blankly ahead. She drew back her Stick and poked him in the stomach. Nothing. No reaction whatsoever.

'That's him sorted,' said Aunt Angry, with a grim smile of satisfaction.

143

'What happens now?' I said uneasily.

'We'll leave him 'ere for a bit. He looks quite decorative, don't ye think? I might move 'im next to the door. He'd make a good coat stand, with his arm stuck up like that.' She caught sight of my face, and chuckled. 'Oh, take that daft look off yer face, I'm only jokin'. I'll clear 'im up later, when there's time. I'll stick him in the room with the rest, then ye can forget about 'im. Ralph, stay 'ere an' keep an eye on 'im. Anyone comes knockin' at the door, give me a Howl. This is the high spot o' my life an' I don't want no interruptions. Wilma, get back in the Ring.'

'Why? Where are we going now?'

'Where d'ye think? Down to the Pool. I want to see what's happenin' in the Pink House. Time for a spot of gloatin'. This is the best bit. No point in goin' to all this trouble unless I gets to gloat, is there?'

'No. I suppose not,' I sighed. And I gave one last, unhappy glance at frozen Prince Brett, then stepped obediently back into the Ring.

17. CHAOS IN THE PINK HOUSE

Seconds later, we were sitting on our Poolside orange boxes, observing what was going on in the Pink House.

Chaos. That's what was going on.

The lounge was all decked out with gaily coloured streamers, balloons and a big banner decorated with hearts and reading: TRUE LOVE CONQUERS ALL. Champagne bottles and glasses were lined up on the sideboard. There were crisps and nibbles and a pile of crackers. There was a big, fancy cake with pink icing.

The Fairies were milling about, tripping over their handbags and wringing their hands. Iris had fainted. Silvia was attempting to bring her round with smelling salts. Lilac and Apricot were weeping loudly into pastel-coloured hankies. Ivy was leaning against a wall, head in her hands. Marigold and Lavender were both having hysterics in a corner.

The Magic Screen was blank.

'My golly,' said Aunt Angry, sounding startled. 'Ye're right, Wilma. They *have* got old. I hardly recognizes 'em. Is that really Lily? The fat one in white? And look at Ivy. She's all bent over.'

'Told you,' I said. 'They're all into knitting and navy-blue handbags and –'

'Shush! I'm tryin' to listen. Hang on, I'll bring up the volume a bit.'

A clamour of loud, anxious voices rang out.

'What's happened? Oh, what in the world has happened?'

'Ring for a leprechaun, Iris needs water!'

'Why? Why's it gone on the blink, today of all days!'

'Somebody kick the wall!'

'I've tried, I've tried!'

'Try the remote again! Who's got the remote?'

There followed more panicky floundering around as everyone searched for the remote.

'How come we're able to watch this?' I asked Aunt Angry.

'Through the mirror. There's one over the mantelpiece, right? Ye should know better than me where the mirror is, ye been there in the flesh.'

'No, I mean, how come we're allowed? I thought you said you couldn't get through to Fairyland on the Pool?'

'Aye. But their defences are down,' explained my great-auntie. 'They've lost their grip. They can't keep tabs on everythin'. They're in shock. Right now, they wouldn't notice if ole Peepin' Tom hisself was lookin' in.'

'But can't they hear us talking?'

'What, with the racket they're makin'? No chance. Just look at 'em, runnin' around like ants with their pants on fire!' She let out a great cackle of laughter. 'This is doin' me a power o' good, Wilma. I ain't enjoyed meself so much since I don't know when.'

Back in the Pool, Tangerine finally found the remote, which — you've guessed it — had fallen down the side of the sofa. With shaking hands, she passed it to Rose, who pointed it at the wall.

It worked. The reception was back. Well, why shouldn't it be? Aunt Angry was no longer scrambling the signal. The wicked deed had already been done.

There was the crossroads, with the sign in place. And there was the silvery Enchanted Path, along which Prince Brett would now be riding, if everything had gone according to plan.

Silence fell — well, there was still a bit of snivelling and nose-blowing going on, but it was silent compared to the ructions of the last minute or two. The Fairies stared hopefully at the Screen. Apart from Iris, who was still out for the count.

'It's empty,' wailed Lilac, shredding a tissue with fidgety fingers.

'But he should be there, on the Path. It's way past two.'

'I can't understand it.'

'If he's not there, where is he? Try his usual haunts, Rose.'

Rose aimed the remote at the Screen. There followed

a quick succession of scene changes. Brett's empty bed; a field containing several archery targets but no Brett; the bar of a quiet country pub in which Brett was conspicuous by his absence; a deserted throne room in which Brett wasn't; an empty stable with no horse and positively no Brett.

'His horse is gone, look,' said Apricot. 'Try the Path again, Rose. Perhaps he's there now.'

Again, the Magic Screen showed the Path, which, of course, remained Brettless.

'Wait!' cried Lavender. 'Move back a bit, Rose. Isn't that his horse? There, look, just before the crossroads. See? It is, isn't it?'

The scene shifted slightly. Back along the road, Prince Brett's horse was standing beneath a tree, swishing its tail and looking somewhat bored.

'She's correct, you know. That's Champion all right. I'd know him anywhere.'

'So where is the dear boy?' moaned Peach. 'If we don't find him, he'll miss the three o'clock deadline. Oh, where is he?'

And then:

'Here!' screeched Aunt Angry, nearly giving me a heart attack. 'He's here, in Starkacre Hall! I've got 'im! I've got 'im and there's nothin' ye can do because he came of his own accord, so there! Ya boo sucks with knobs on! Ha, ha, ha, ha, ha!'

She hauled herself to her feet and waved her Stick around, beside herself with malicious glee.

'Shush, Auntie,' I hissed, trying to pull her back down. 'They'll hear you.'

'Good!' screamed my great-auntie. 'I wants 'em to!'

It was too late, anyway. Twelve silent faces were turned directly towards us. Iris had recovered from her faint. The drama was too good to miss.

'Well, well, well,' said Rose slowly. 'If it isn't Angria.'

'Yep!' squawked my auntie. ''Tis me all right! I got the better of ye at last, didn't I? Got a bloomin' great party planned, aincha? I notice ye didn't invite me. But I don't care, because 'tis all gone belly up, ain't it? Now who's celebratin', eh? Me! See, look? I'm dancin'! See me dancin'?'

Much to my amazement, she was. Despite the new shoes, she was shuffling around on the spot, kicking up her old feet in manic glee. Mother's cream must be *really* good.

In the Magic Pool, the twelve Fairies were watching in grim silence. Twenty-four eyes were trained on her. Good Fairies they might be, but there was something very scary about their expressions.

'Sit down, Aunt Angry,' I muttered. 'Enough's enough. You've done your gloating, let's leave it at that, eh?'

But she wouldn't. Talk about rubbing it in. She carried on, jeering and crowing and capering about– then, to my horror, she did something really, *really* rude. She turned her back to the Pool, bent over, flipped up her skirt and presented her bloomer-clad bottom, while simultaneously blowing a huge raspberry.

This proved too much for the Fairies.

'Right, girls,' said Rose, through gritted teeth. 'I think we've seen quite enough. Are we all ready?'

'Ready!' came the grim chorus. Every one of them

reached for her handbag. Those who were seated stood up. There came the sound of a dozen little clicks as they simultaneously opened their handbags and withdrew twelve Wands.

'On the count of three,' said Rose. 'One – two –'

They raised their Wands.

'*Three!*'

The Magic Pool went dark.

And the dungeon suddenly became very, very crowded.

18. THE CONFRONTATION

You know how untidy Aunt Angry's lab is, with loads of clutter all over the place. Add to that twelve Fairies, in stiff net frocks and bulky woollies, each carrying a large, navy-blue handbag and a Wand.

They arrived quietly, with no fuss. They simply faded in, each one neatly occupying the bits of floor space which hadn't been taken up with rubbish.

Aunt Angry stopped capering. She just stood there, hand resting lightly on the knob of her Stick. She looked proud and triumphant. You'd never have known that her feet were hurting like blazes. She had an air of defiant dignity which, to my mind, beat crowing and dancing hands down.

They stared at each other then, my great-auntie and

the Twelve Good Fairies. I took a step or two backwards and tried to blend into the shadows – not because I was frightened, but because I knew that this had nothing to do with me. This was war, no doubt about it. There would be harsh words spoken. There would be accusations and a lot of shouting. Finally, there would be fireworks. Magical fireworks. The sort where people can get hurt.

All right, I admit it. I *was* a bit frightened. For the first time since my arrival, I took out my own Wand and held it in my sweaty palm, all ready to use if things got really hairy. Better safe than sorry.

There was a long, long silence. And then Lilac spoke.

'Brrr,' she said. 'It's bloomin' chilly down here.'

The rest of the Fairies nodded agreement. There was a lot of shawl adjustment and theatrical shivering.

'You keeps it too hot at your place,' snapped Great-Aunt Angria defensively. 'I seen it. I knows.'

'I'm surprised you don't catch cold, Angria,' observed Primrose. 'You should put in double glazing, dear.'

'What, at the prices they charge?' said Aunt Angry. 'I'd sooner freeze.'

I couldn't believe my ears. Here were ancient enemies confronting each other for the first time in one hundred and sixteen years – *and they were discussing the merits of double glazing*!

'Anyway,' said Aunt Angry. 'This won't get the baby bathed. Are we gonna do this or are we gonna stand around all night discussin' my heatin' arrangements?'

'By all means,' said Ivy briskly. 'That's what we're here for.'

'First off, who said ye could come 'ere?' demanded

Aunt Angry. Her hair was stirring now. 'I don't take kindly to uninvited guests. Ye're s'posed to get permission before ye cross my threshold. From me.'

Ooer. Things were getting nasty. Perhaps there was going to be a proper showdown after all.

'True,' said Rose sweetly. 'But you've been doing plenty of snooping of your own, haven't you, dear? Using your Pool on us and sending spies along?'

With one accord, they all turned and looked at me. I gave a sickly grin and fingered my Wand.

'It was only the one spy,' said Aunt Angry. 'My great-niece Wilma. Veronica's daughter. Come out of there, Wilma, and say hello in a proper manner.'

'Hello,' I said, stepping forward. 'Sorry about the – er –'

'No ye're not!' scolded Aunt Angry. 'Never say sorry! Ye're not sorry about nothin'. You was just doin' what you was told. She's a good girl, really,' she told the Fairies. Rather to my surprise, her voice held a certain amount of pride. 'Comin' along nicely. She's got her Grade Three. Studyin' for Grade Four, ain't ye, Wilma? This is her work experience.'

'Oh, right,' nodded all the Fairies. 'That's nice.'

'She looks a bit like you, Angria,' added Iris. 'Around the eyes.'

'Bad hair, too,' nodded Tangerine.

Honestly. That *was* below the belt.

'Anyway,' said Rose suddenly. 'Angria's right. We'd better get this thing settled once and for all. Not to beat about the bush, Angria, what have you done with our Prince?'

'He's upstairs, in the hall, doin' a fine impression of a coat stand,' said Aunt Angry tartly. 'I'm thinkin' of hangin' me hat on him later.'

'It's against the Law, you know,' said Tangerine. 'What you just done.'

'No it ain't. Ye interfered with my curse, so I can interfere with yer spell. Tit for tat. 'Tis allowed. Ye haven't read the fine print. I should know, I been lookin' for a loophole for the last hundred years.'

'I think you'll find you're out of order, dear,' chipped in Primrose. '*A good spell is equal to the sum of three curses.* It states that quite clearly in the Rules and Statutes. Item five, paragraph seven.'

'Ah!' said Aunt Angry. 'But what about item twenty-nine, clause three? *A foiled curse entitles the curser to one free attempt at retaliation provided no direct interference is involved.* Direct! Get my meanin'?'

'I don't believe that,' said Marigold. 'I don't think it says that at all.'

'Tell you what,' said Lavender. 'Let's check it in the book. Have you got a copy lying around, Angria?'

''Course,' said Aunt Angry. 'Hold my Stick a minute, Wilma. I need both hands free for this.'

I took her Stick. She held out her hands, palms up.

Pop!

Suddenly, she was holding a large, heavy, leather-bound book which I recognized as *Ye Book of Magickal Law.* All twelve Fairies surged forward and crowded round Aunt Angry, trying to look over her shoulder.

'We'll take it over to the bench,' said Aunt Angry. 'The light's better over there. And there's a magnifyin' glass. I think ye'll find I'm right …'

They all moved off to the bench, leaving me alone and ignored next to the Magic Pool with Aunt Angry's Stick.

Cautiously, I touched the silver knob. It didn't give me a shock this time. Perhaps it recognized me as family. I could feel the life in it, though. It hummed and buzzed in my hand. It was quite thrilling, actually, handling all that pent-up Power. I wondered what it would feel like to release it.

I glanced over at my great-auntie, who was seated at her bench with the book open. Her back was to me. Nobody was looking. They were all too busy arguing about the finer points of the Law.

I held out the Stick over the Magic Pool. Just as an experiment, to see if anything would happen.

It did. The water began to boil. I had seen Aunt Angry muttering under her breath when she did this. I didn't know what she said, so I decided to improvise.

'The Path,' I whispered. 'Let me see the Enchanted Path.'

Instantly, the Enchanted Path appeared, leading away from the crossroads. The empty path along which Prince Brett should be …

But wait a minute. It wasn't empty. Someone was walking along it. A wild-looking bearded man wearing a tattered toga and with a lopsided circle of vine leaves on his head. He had a vague, bewildered air about him. Even as I watched, he reached inside his toga, took out a flask, unscrewed the cap and took a little nip.

My eyes nearly shot out of my head. I recognized that portly figure! Well, I ought to. After all, I'd seen it at the dinner table back home enough times, tucking into thirds of everything. But whatever was he doing wandering along an Enchanted Path, a zillion miles and four dimensions away from home? And why was he looking so scruffy and confused?

'Excuse me?' I called excitedly. Everyone ignored me. They were too busy turning pages and arguing about clause this and paragraph that.

'Auntie!' I shouted. 'There's something I think you should see.'

'What *is* it, Wilma? Can't ye see we're busy ...'

She turned around in her chair. Her brow darkened.

'Oi! What are you playin' at? 'Ave you been usin' my Stick? Are ye crazy, girl? That Stick's only to be used by me, unless I gives my express permi—'

'Who's that?' broke in Apricot, who was nearest to the Pool. She pointed. 'There's somebody walking down our Path!'

Seconds later, the Pool was surrounded.

'What's he doing there?'

'Who's that?'

'It's a tramp!'

'Get him off the Path!'

'Quick! Zap him!'

Twelve handbags clicked open simultaneously. There was a united rummaging for Wands. This was too much. I had to do something.

'You leave him alone!' I shouted. 'He's *not* a tramp. He's my uncle and you're not to hurt him. Tell them, Aunt Angry. They mustn't zap him, must they?'

Aunt Angria was now standing at my side, watching

closely as Uncle Bacchus wandered on up the Path. He had come quite a way along it. The signpost was now far behind him. Up ahead, in the distance, was a great, brambly hedge. I thought I caught a glimpse of a thin tower rising behind it. This must be the hedge surrounding Beauty's castle.

'Wait,' she said. 'Leave him be a minute. I wants to look at him. Let's bring the sound up.'

She snatched her Stick from my hand and fiddled with the knob. Uncle Bacchus's deep bass voice came rumbling from the Pool. He was singing.

'*Show me the way to go home*,' sang Uncle Bacchus, taking another little swig. '*I'm tired and I want a big kebab ...*'

'That's my nephew, that is,' said Aunt Angry. 'Ain't seen him in the flesh for years. I remember when Grimelza got him from the adoption agency, when he were nobbut a toddler. A right little rascal he was. Cute as a button. O' course, nobody invited me over to meet him but I used to watch him in me Scryin' Glass from time to time. On nights when I was feelin' a bit – low.'

There was something sad in the way she said this. I put a hand on her arm, but she shook it off impatiently and gave me a fierce glare.

'Well, he's not cute now, dear,' pointed out Rose. 'He's a smelly old tramp and we're not having him kissing our Beauty. Not when there's a perfectly good Prince upstairs.'

'He's not usually that grubby,' I butted in, defending my poor old Uncle Bacchus whom, as I've told you, I'm very fond of. He slips me the occasional fiver and takes his false teeth out at parties. He's kind and enjoys a good laugh. Beauty could do worse.

Although I had to admit he *was* a bit old for someone who was only a hundred and sixteen.

'Even so,' said Rose. 'Who'd like to wake up to a smacker from *that* whiskery old goat? Admit it, Angria. It wouldn't be right.'

The rest of the Fairies nodded agreement.

'Ah, what do I care about right and wrong?' snapped Aunt Angria. Her hair was stirring. 'Nothin' ever happened right for me. Stop yer bleatin', I'm sick of the lot o' ye.'

She fiddled with the knob of her Stick and, instantly, the Pool went dark. Uncle Bacchus was cut off mid-warble.

'There,' she said. 'Enough of that. Fate's takin' a hand now. What will be will be. 'Tis out of our hands.'

'No it isn't,' argued Rose. 'Fate may be taking a hand, but that doesn't mean we can't affect the final outcome. Face it, Angria. Beauty's going to wake up. The only question now is, who's going to wake her? A nice young man with lovely hair and good prospects or a daft old wine god? Yes, yes, I know he's your nephew, but there are limits.'

'You can't take us all on, you know,' chipped in Marigold.

'Yes I can,' snapped my great-auntie. 'I'll win too.'

'But at what cost?' asked Iris. 'Come on, dear. You know it makes sense.'

All eyes were on my auntie. What would she do? Give in gracefully and admit defeat? Or try to muck things up to the very last? What she did took me by surprise.

She turned to me.

'What do you say, Wilma?' she said. 'What shall I do? Let ye be the judge. I'd certainly value yer opinion. Ye're a clever girl, with yer Grade Three an' all that. Ye must have learned somethin' from yer work experience. Now's yer chance ter shine. Ye know what's at stake here.'

I did, too. Her reputation. It was all she had. On the other hand, some things had to be said. All eyes were on me. What was I to do? This was my big moment.

'Can I have a word in private?' I asked.

'By all means. Talk amongst yerselves!' she ordered. And we stepped to one side.

'Well,' I said slowly. 'The way I see it is this. You can't just pass the buck and leave it all to Fate. Fate's not responsible for what happens next. You are. You started it, you finish it.'

'Point taken. But how shall I end it? Ye saw what they did, back then. Ganged up on me and made me lose face. Smug know-alls, with their fancy get-up. Showin' off.'

'But that was *years* ago. Why still hold a grudge? They've changed, Auntie. You can see that. They're nicer now. And why shouldn't Beauty marry Brett? I mean, I love Uncle Bacchus, but really! I don't think he'd make a good husband.'

'Uh huh.' Aunt Angry considered. 'So what ye're sayin' is, I should back down. Tell 'em all is forgiven and forgotten, eh? That I've seen the light. That I'm older and wiser and in my very wise wisdom I've decided that Prince Brett can kiss her, they can fall in love and live happily ever after. An' let's all be happy 'cos I'm too old

159

an' tired for wickedness and from now on I'll be leavin' it up to people who are younger an' smarter than me. Right?'

'Yes,' I said happily. 'I'd say that just about covers it.'

Rather pleased with myself, I waited smugly for her to do just that. She'd asked for my advice and I'd given it. She'd seen reason. All because of me.

You know what she said?

'Bull-doos to that,' she said. And raised her Stick.

Thunder cracked. It began to get dark. The Good Fairies muttered among themselves. Wands were being raised. And I realized that, despite all my efforts, I'd failed. There was to be a Magical showdown after all. If my great-auntie won, Beauty and Brett were doomed. If the Fairies won – that would be the end of my auntie. Either way, there would be no happy ending.

Oh well. At least I'd learned an important lesson. You can talk common sense until you're blue in the face, but in the end, people do as they like.

And then something very unexpected happened.

19. UNEXPECTED VISITORS

'Hello, everybody!' said a fresh, familiar voice. 'Hello, Aunt Angria, dear. I thought I'd drop by to see if you've finished with our Wilma yet. My word, it's crowded in here. I do hope this isn't a bad time.'

It was Mother! She stepped out from a shadowy corner. I had no idea how long she had been there. She had a bunch of dark red roses in one hand and a large box of Dark Nibbles in the other.

I'd never been so glad to see her in my life. Whatever happened next, it wasn't my responsibility.

'Mother!' I cried. I would have rushed to embrace her, but there were too many Fairies in the way. Anyway, she wasn't looking at me. She was looking at my Great-Aunt Angria.

'Well, well,' said my auntie dryly. 'If it ain't Veronica. Meet my niece, everybody. My sister Grimelza's daughter. The current Queen of the Night.'

The Fairies nodded and dropped wobbly little curtsies. Mother responded with a deep bow.

'So ye've finally come to see me,' said Aunt Angry. 'After all this time.'

'I know,' said Mother, with a little sigh. She glided through the crowd, not touching anyone or tripping over anything, though I haven't a clue how she managed it. She reached Aunt Angry, bent and kissed her cheek, then placed the gifts in her arms.

'I'm *so* sorry, Auntie. I just don't know where the years have gone. I kept meaning to get in touch, but ...'

'Ye didn't,' Aunt Angry finished off for her.

'No,' admitted Mother, with a rueful little sigh. 'I didn't. Pressures of work, three girls to bring up, you know how it is. Of course, you could always have come and visited *us*.'

'I never got no invitation.'

'You don't need an invitation!' cried Mother. 'You're family. Anyway,' she added brightly, 'I'm here now. And it seems I've arrived right in the middle of some sort of – er – lovely social gathering. Won't you introduce me to your friends?'

She smiled around at the twelve old Fairies, who had been watching this exchange with interest.

'They're no friends o' mine,' declared my auntie. 'These are me ancient enemies, the Twelve Good Fairies, and they ain't here to play Bingo.'

'How do you do, ladies?' said Mother politely. 'I've

heard of your reputation. Of course, we're on opposite sides of the fence, so to speak, but it's always good to build bridges, don't you think?'

The Fairies murmured agreement. Well, they would do. They were *good* Fairies. They believed in things like manners and compromise.

'So, tell me, Auntie,' continued Mother. 'How are your feet? Did the cream work?'

'Aye,' admitted Aunt Angry. 'It was good stuff, Veronica. First time I've worn heels for years. These smell nice.' She sniffed the roses. Then she examined the box of chocolates. 'Oooh,' she said. 'Dark Nibbles. My favourite.'

'I prefer the white ones myself,' said Lily. Adding quickly: 'Although I don't say no to either.'

'I can't abide the toffee ones,' muttered Iris. 'They plays havoc with me false teeth.'

A little discussion broke out about the merits of various types of chocolate. I was beginning to feel impatient. Things had got off course a bit. Everyone seemed to have forgotten all about Beauty and Brett and the critical timing. Nobody was interested in what was happening to Uncle Bacchus either. I suddenly remembered that Mother wasn't even aware that he had been found. I opened my mouth to tell her the glad news, and then –

'*Oooooooooooooowwwwwwwww!*'

Ralph's Howl rang out from somewhere up above.

'Darn it!' shouted Aunt Angry. '*Now* what? *More* blasted visitors?'

'Are you expecting anyone, dear?' enquired Ivy.

"'Course not! I dunno, you waits for a hundred years then they all comes at once!'

'**Ooooooooooooooooowwwww!**'

Another of Ralph's specials, more urgent this time.

'All right, all right, I'm comin'!' Aunt Angry paused and glared around. 'Gotta go up to the hall,' she snapped. 'Won't be a minute. Then we'll carry on with the main business.'

'That's all right, dear, you take your time. In fact, we'll come with you,' said Primrose. 'It might be less chilly. More room, too.'

They all vanished then, including Mother. It was brilliant. They just weren't there any more. I was left all alone in the deserted dungeon. Hopefully, I waved my Wand and muttered a Relocation Spell, but nothing happened. I just don't have the knack. It takes years to perfect something like that.

Stairs again. Goody.

Mercifully, the dungeon stairs open out into the hall, so it didn't take me that long. They had a head start on me, of course, so I missed the actual opening of the main door. I knew who was there, though. I heard the voices.

'*Mother!*' That was Scarlettine, all shrill and attention-grabbing. 'I've been trying to contact you *all day*! Daddy said I'd find you here. Is your Ball turned off or something?'

'*Mother!*' That was Frostia, all haughty and accusing. 'These dreadful builders, you won't *believe* what they're demanding now! They want me to provide little *huts* so they can eat their lunch out of the blizzards ...'

'Now then, darlings,' came Mother's voice. 'It's lovely to see you, and I'll hear all about it later, but aren't you forgetting your manners? This is your Great-Aunt Angria. And these are the Twelve Good Fairies.'

'Hello,' said Scarlettine disinterestedly.

'Hello,' honked Frostia. 'Look, Mother, I'm being *ripped off*! Can they do that to a queen?'

'Shut up, Frosty, I'm first!' squawked Scarlettine. 'Oh, Mother, I've had such a *dreadful* time. The engagement to Black Jack Kipper's off. He turned out to have a wife in every port. My heart is quite bro– Oh!' She gasped. 'Who's this?'

She had suddenly noticed Prince Brett, standing by the door with his arm raised.

'That's Prince Brett,' I said, advancing into the hall and making my way through the Fairies. 'Keep your hands off him. He's Beauty's, not yours.'

'Shut up, Wilma, who asked you? He's rather dishy, isn't he? Is he always like this? He's under a spell, isn't he? Who did it to him?'

I looked at Aunt Angry, expecting her to claim responsibility and hopefully put Scarlettine in her place, but she was too busy examining the pictures on the back of the chocolate box.

'Can somebody shut the door?' piped up Tangerine suddenly. 'It's very draughty in here.'

Ralph, who had been taking a back seat all this time, brightened up. He trotted across and was about to nose it shut, when his ears went back and he let out yet another warning Howl.

'*Ooooooooooooowwwwwww!*'

'I don't believe this,' said Aunt Angry testily. 'Can't a party be left alone to try a chocolate for two minutes? What is it *now*?'

'There'sh a caravan outshide, Mishtresh,' said Ralph, all eager. 'Shall I chashe it off?'

There was, too. It was parked in the courtyard. A plump donkey stood between the shafts, staring in at us. Aunt Maud and New Uncle Frank stood on either side of the step, holding out their arms to support Grandma as she climbed down. They looked rather tired, I noticed.

Grandma didn't, though. She looked just fine. She was wearing a frilly crimson skirt, a fringed shawl and huge hoop earrings. A spotted scarf was knotted over her hairnet. She was holding her Stick.

'Get off!' she shouted, smacking away the helpful hands. 'I can do it meself, I don't need you!'

Now, where had I heard that before?

I looked at Aunt Angry. She had lost interest in the chocolates. She had dumped them, together with the flowers, on the edge of the dais. Her face was a mask of – what? Anger? Maybe. Surprise? A bit. And something else that I can't quite put a name to.

'Grim?' she said. 'Is that you?' She took a couple of steps towards the door. Everyone moved back to let her pass.

Grandma had reached the threshold. Her eyes went past the assembled company. It was as though they weren't there. She was staring at my Great-Aunt Angria. My Great-Aunt Angria was staring right back. Now they were together in the flesh, you could see that they were as alike as two peas in a pod. Apart from the hair and the clothes, of course.

Silence fell. A long, long silence. Even Scarlettine shut up for once. I crossed my fingers behind my back, willing them to fall into each other's arms like people do in stories. But they didn't.

'You daft or somethin'?' snapped Grandma. 'O' course it's me. Are you gonna invite me in or what? Ah, what the heck, I'm comin' anyway. Who needs an invitation?'

And she hobbled over the threshold. *Without* being invited. I held my breath.

Nothing happened. Well, nothing except a row.

'You haven't changed much,' sneered Grandma. 'Still goin' in for the flyin' hair effect, I see.'

'At least I've still *got* hair,' said Aunt Angry sharply. Her dander was up. Great coils of the stuff were flapping around her shoulders. 'At least I don't have no *perm*. And I might have known *ye'd* show up when I got chocolates.'

They hobbled a bit closer to each other.

'What's all these Fairies doin' here?' enquired Grandma. 'You gone soft or summit?'

The Fairies bridled a bit at this, but no one said anything. There comes a time when you have to accept that you are just an extra, and let the stars of the show get on with it.

'Wouldn't *ye* like to know. Anyway, what's with the daft get-up?' Aunt Angry cast a withering eye over Grandma's eccentric attire.

'Didn't they tell you?' Grandma twirled her skirt and preened a little. 'I bin to a Gypsy Convention. Thought it was time I had a bit of fun for a change.'

'Ye shouldn't have fun at your age,' scoffed her twin.

'Yeah, yeah. You're just put out because you never got invited.'

'No I ain't,' argued Aunt Angry. 'Mutton dressed as lamb, I calls it.'

'You do? I calls it ex-Queen o' the Night dressed as a fun-lovin' gypsy!' shot back Grandma.

'Ye had to get that in, didn't ye?' said Aunt Angry bitterly. 'Ye just can't help rubbin' it in after all these years.'

'Fact remains that I'm queen!'

'*Was* queen. *Was.* But ye ain't now. Ye're retired, remember? Just as well. Ye was always lousy at the job.'

'Still got me Stick, though,' said Grandma dangerously. They were nearly nose to nose. Their knuckles were clenched tightly on the knobs of their identical Sticks.

'Aye,' snarled Aunt Angry, hair lashing like a haystack in a high wind. 'An' I still got mine. An' it's not just for show, neither. Ye might be the ex-Queen o' the Night, Grimelza, *but I am the Thirteenth Faerie!*'

Outside, the obligatory thunder crashed. Little green sparks were beginning to crackle up and down the length of their Sticks. Smoke arose from where the two tips touched the floor.

I almost butted in at this point. Well, somebody had to try and save them from themselves. But I felt Mother's cool hand on my shoulder, and I sank into anxious silence.

Oh dear. Things weren't going at all well. Age might make you mellow, but it doesn't stop you arguing with your sister, apparently. They had just taken up where they left off when they were kids. In thousands of years' time,

Frostia, Scarlettine and I will be like this.

Then something happened that I think took everyone by surprise.

'Here, Grim!' said Aunt Angry suddenly in quite a normal voice. 'Changin' the subject. I know what I was gonna tell ye. Guess who Wilma bumped into? Chef Basin. Remember him, when we was kids? He left because we always used to say his name wrong on purpose.' She gave a little snort of laughter.

'What, old Chef Basin? Never!' said Grandma, astonished. '*Did* you, Wilma?'

'Er – yes, Grandma,' I piped up. 'He's cooking for the Fairies now.'

'Is that right?' gasped Grandma, amazed.

The watching Fairies all nodded, confirming that this was indeed the case.

'He's come down in the world, then,' remarked Grandma rudely. The Fairies tutted and whispered among themselves.

'That's what I said,' chortled Aunt Angry.

'I wonder if he still does that soufflé?'

They both raised an enquiring eyebrow at the Fairies, who nodded again, confirming that he did, indeed, still do the soufflé.

'But we prefer the trifle,' added Lily.

'Oh, yes, well. He does do a lovely trifle,' agreed Aunt Angry. 'I remember the trifle, don't you, Grim?'

'Oh aye,' nodded Grandma. 'Very generous with the sherry. Talkin' of sherry, I could do with a drop.'

For the first time since their arrival, Aunt Maud spoke up.

'Do you really think you should, Mama? With your tummy?'

'Don't, Mama,' begged Mother. 'Maud's right. After all that camp-fire food, I really don't think you should be –'

'Oh, I don't know. Might settle her,' chipped in Tangerine suddenly. 'Although I prefer elderberry wine meself,' she added.

'I might have a bottle o' that somewhere,' said Aunt Angry vaguely. 'Dunno about sherry, though.'

'I've been drinking rum,' jumped in Scarlettine, finally unable to take the lack of attention any longer. 'I've been on the high seas,' she announced to the room. 'They drink a lot of rum there.'

Honestly. Was I the only one finding this bizarre? Here they all were, discussing trivia, when elsewhere, a huge drama was unfolding involving ancient curses and sleeping princesses and what have you. And time was running –

'Ahhh!' I screamed, pointing at the huge egg-timer on the platform. 'Look! Look! Time's running out!'

The top bit of the timer was almost empty. There couldn't have been more than a thimbleful of sand left.

I gazed at the clock. The big hand was over three-quarters of the way round the face. The little hand had almost reached three.

There were only ten more minutes to go!

20. THE KISS

'Well, Angria, it's up to you now,' said Rose. 'You can do the decent thing and put matters to right or carry on being a stubborn old woman and ruin two lovely young people's lives and go down in history as a spoilsport. Which is it to be?'

All eyes turned towards my great-auntie. Then, rather surprisingly, Grandma spoke up.

'Ah, leave her alone,' she snapped. 'Who asked you anyway? You're talkin' to my sister who just happens to be the Thirteenth Faerie. Show some respect.'

'Thanks, Grim,' said Aunt Angry. 'You tell 'er.'

'I just did.'

'But it isn't right!' argued Rose. 'It has to be a Prince who wakes her!'

'Ah, but ye never *said* that,' Aunt Angry told her smugly. '*Be woken by a kiss,* you said. You never stipulated *who* was to do the kissin'. Muck about with a person's curse, ye oughta make sure ye gets the words right. Right, Grim?'

'Absolutely!' agreed Grandma. 'Bunch o' bloomin' amateurs.'

Rose went pink. Well, pinker.

'All right,' she said. 'All right, so I wasn't as careful as I might have been. I was young and a bit overconfident. We all were back then. But we're older and wiser now. Time to bury our differences and make this thing come out the way it's supposed to ...'

'Yeah, yeah,' muttered Aunt Angry. 'I've heard it all before.'

'... and furthermore,' Fairy Rose went on, 'and just to show there's no ill feeling, the girls and I would like to present you with this.'

She unclipped her handbag, reached in and withdrew a large, silver envelope decorated with pink butterflies. Written in pink was *Angria, the Thirteenth Faerie.* Formally, she handed it to my auntie.

'What's this?' muttered Aunt Angry, staring down at it.

'It's your invitation to our Awakening Party. I forgot to post it, but now I can give it to you by hand.'

'An invitation? What – for me?'

'Yes.'

'What – to your place?'

'Yes. It's an historic occasion. We all agreed you should come.'

'See this, Grim?' said Aunt Angry, turning to

Grandma. She sounded surprised, excited and – touched. Yes, touched. 'It's a proper invite! For me. With me name on it.'

'So I see,' said Grandma. 'Might be a laugh. Are you gonna go?'

There was a silence. It seemed to go on for ever. I had to do something. I stepped forward and put my hand on Aunt Angry's arm. For once, she didn't shake it off.

'Go on,' I said. 'Look, I know you'll do what you want whatever anyone says. But it's a proper invite. It'd be rude to refuse. Besides, think what a feather it'd be in their caps. To be able to say that the Thirteenth Faerie came to their party.'

That did it. She gave a brisk nod.

'Stand back!' she ordered. Everyone shuffled out of the way as she raised her Stick and aimed it at Prince Brett. Scarlettine was standing right next to him, poking at his muscles with a long, red talon. I hoped she would get caught in the cross-fire but, sadly, she gave a little squeal and jumped aside just in time. A stream of green sparks shot out and splashed all over Prince Brett.

Instantly, he came back to life. He blinked, flexed his shoulder muscles, stared around and said:

'What the … ?'

Then he vanished, just like that – and in his place stood dear old Uncle Bacchus, swaying and scratching his head and looking highly confused.

'Uncle!' I shouted, and ran to hug him. He smelled a bit salty, for some reason.

'*Bacchus!*' cried Mother. 'There you are! Where have you *been?*'

'Where's the Prince?' all the Fairies were asking. 'Where's Brett?'

'Should be hacking his way through the brambles by now,' said Aunt Angry. 'Muscles like that, won't take him long. I've given him a bit of extra speed too, so he should make it to the castle and up to the tower room in double-quick time.'

At this, a spontaneous round of applause broke out from the assembled company, apart from Scarlettine, who obviously had him marked out for herself, and Frostia, who was trying to avoid the attentions of Ralph. There was something about her chilly look that reminded him of chasing sledges through the snow.

'So,' said Rose. 'That's sorted. Shall we go back to the Pink House and watch on the Magic Screen? Your relations are most welcome, of course, Angria. It's warmer back there, no offence intended. And we're all set up for the party.'

'Will there be Chef Basin's trifle?' asked Aunt Angry. She hobbled to the dais and picked up her roses and box of chocolates.

'Of course.'

'Then what are we waitin' for?'

Suddenly, I found myself alone in the great hall. Even Ralph had vanished. It seemed that everyone present had mastered the art of Instant Relocation, apart from me. I couldn't believe it. After all my hard work, I wasn't even going to see the final outcome. I could have wept. I would have, too, except that Mother suddenly reappeared, right next to me.

'Sorry, darling,' she said. 'I'd forgotten you haven't

done Personal Transportation yet. You've done terribly well and I'm very pleased with you. Give me a hug.'

I went to embrace her. As she folded me into her shadowy arms, I had a brief impression of whirling, black space filled with a million stars –

And then we were in the hot, crowded lounge in the Pink House. Everyone was clustered around the Magic Screen, watching events unfold. Sadly, we arrived at the back and Frostia was right in front of me. She's six feet tall, so I missed the Kiss. Not that I cared that much. I'm not a great one for kissing. I knew it had happened, though, because of the great cheer that went up.

When I finally managed to squeeze past Frostia and get a glimpse of what was happening, Beauty was already sitting up on the pile of flax gazing into Brett's eyes. Brett was looking at her in the way I look at a bag of doughnuts, so that was all right.

From all around came the sound of popping champagne corks. Aunt Angry had opened her box of chocolates and was sharing them, rather grudgingly, I thought. The Fairies, Uncle Bacchus and Grandma were already getting stuck into the cake. Ralph had contrived to accidentally on purpose knock over a plate of cheese straws and was wolfing them down, ha, ha. Scarlettine and Frostia had finally cornered Mother and were bleating on about their own paltry problems, totally unconcerned that they had just witnessed the triumphal ending of an ancient grudge which doubtless would be talked about for centuries to come.

I wandered over to the sideboard, grabbed a plateful of Twiglets and threw myself down on to a footstool. On the Magic Screen, Brett and Beauty had descended the turret stairs and were walking past a couple of bewildered-looking guards, who were too busy picking spiders out of their beards to stand to attention. Not that Brett and Beauty cared. It was clear that they were in love. Brett and Beauty, I mean, not the guards.

'Don't fill yourself up on rubbish, Wilma,' said Mother, gliding past me with Frostia and Scarlettine in her wake, still clamouring for her attention. 'There's a proper feast waiting, apparently.'

There was, too. It was all set out on a long table in the (pink) banqueting hall. I must say, the Fairies really know how to lay a table. It groaned with cold meats, pies, sausage rolls, little bits of cheese and pineapple on sticks, tiny sandwiches with the crusts cut off and a choice of fillings. There was a lovely soufflé too. And as for the sweet stuff – well! Biscuits, cakes, buns, doughnuts, jam tarts, chocolate rolls, meringues, eclairs, jelly, ice-cream and the best trifle I've ever tasted, although I wouldn't say that to Mrs Pudding.

We were waited upon by the leprechauns, of course. Shaun gave a bit of a start when he saw me sitting next to Mother near the top of the table, but didn't say anything. I suppose he's used to surprises, what with having nine children.

I ate a *lot*. I admit it. In three days, all I'd had to eat were chocolate biscuits, doughnuts, sugar lumps, chocolate eclairs, mince pies, porridge and leprechaun broth. Actually, when you write it down, it looks like quite a lot. But I ate most of it at the beginning and the last day's fare had been very frugal. I had a lot

of catching up to do. Here's what I stuffed my face
with:

14 Twiglets
2 large pieces of cake
3 portions of soufflé
6 mini sausage rolls
2 doughnuts
16 cheese and pineapple thingies
14 sandwiches (well, they were small)
1 plate of pink jelly and strawberry ice-cream
3 helpings of trifle
4 pink milkshakes

Mother kept staring darkly and shaking her head, but
I pretended not to notice.

Uncle Bacchus ate loads too. So did the twelve Good
Fairies. So did Grandma and Great-Aunt Angria, who sat
side by side mumbling to each other about ye olde tymes
while still managing to get stuck into the trifle. I was
rather hoping there might be a meeting between them
and Chef Basin but, wisely, he kept out of the way. Too
ashamed to show his face, perhaps. Personally, I'm glad he
doesn't cook for us. He's just too *emotional*. At least you
know where you are with Mrs Pudding.

Aunt Maud was the only one who ate the salad. New
Uncle Frank sat and silently, methodically, consumed
everything going. Mother picked politely at a bowl of
radishes, Scarlettine ate apples and Frostia had ice cubes
with a dash. (Of water, in case you're wondering.)

Much to my relief, Ralph didn't join us at the table.

He had a bowl on the floor and a personal leprechaun whose job it was to keep it topped up.

At the end of the meal, when I was on the point of explosion, Rose proposed a toast.

'Raise your glasses, everyone,' she announced. 'A toast to Angria, the Thirteenth Faerie, who –' She broke off. I held my breath, hoping desperately that she wouldn't mention anything about my auntie coming to see the error of her ways. I didn't think that would go down at all well. But she didn't.

'– who showed enough wisdom and common sense to come to a compromise,' she finished, and I breathed again.

Then my great-auntie spoke.

'I got a toast too,' she said.

There was instant silence. She rose to her feet and looked around. I looked down the table. Everyone's face wore a wary expression. After all, this was the perfect moment for her to revert to type and lash out with a surprise, last-minute curse. I mean, that was her style. You could have heard a pin drop as she raised her glass.

'To Wilma,' she said simply. 'Thanks for the help, girl. And the company. I've enjoyed havin' ye round the last three days. Ye're a chip off the old block, and I can't say fairer than that. Ye've done a good job with that girl, Veronica. She shows a lot of promise.'

'Hear, hear,' chimed in Grandma. 'To Wilma.'

'To Wilma,' murmured the assembled company, all except Frostia and Scarlettine who exchanged sneering glances and began to whisper in each other's ears. Plotting against me as usual.

As if I cared!

We didn't hang about after the feast was over. The Fairies were all for returning to the lounge to finish off the champagne and watch a re-run of the whole soppy business, starting with Brett fighting through the brambles, which we had missed first time round – but, rather to my relief, Mother announced that she had to get back to get ready for the Round. Also, Grandma needed her indigestion tablets, which were back at the Ancestral Halls. So we missed the firework display and the dancing and the bells ringing out all over Fairyland, etc., etc.

I didn't mind. I'd had enough of the whole thing by then. I wanted to get back home. I was eager to see Daddy and felt it was time to be reunited with my toothbrush, which as you know I hadn't packed.

Besides, you can have too much trifle.

21. LOOSE ENDS

Back at the Ancestral Halls, there was bad news and good news. The bad news, relayed to us by Peevish, was that the mulch had turned out to be the *wrong sort* and that Daddy had gone off to get some of the right stuff. The good news was that Alvis had returned from his fishing trip. Hooray! I simply couldn't wait to see him.

He also informed us that there was actual food back on the menu. In fact, even now, Mrs Pudding was humming away happily in the kitchen, preparing yet another celebration feast.

Yes! *Denzil had returned!* Apparently, he had somehow made his way back through a zillion miles and four dimensions into Mrs Pudding's arms in the small hours of the morning, all wet and forlorn and desperate for his fish heads.

I'm going to enter him for *The Guinness Book of Records*. To my certain knowledge, no cat has ever travelled that far, including the one in *The Incredible Journey*.

That was it, really. Nothing else had happened in my absence.

It was good to be home. Well, it was until Frostia and Scarlettine started picking on me. Grandma and Aunt Angry (yes – of course she was with us) wandered off somewhere, Mother went to butter up Mrs Pudding, Uncle Bacchus found a sofa and went to sleep, Aunt Maud and New Uncle Frank went to clean out the caravan (which had mysteriously returned of its own accord) and Ralph went off to sniff out the territory and see if there were any small girls in red cloaks to irritate. I think he went to the kitchens first, because I heard a lot of distant screaming.

That left me and my two sisters. Guess what we did? Right. Had a row.

'I suppose you think you're someone special now, *Wilma*!' (Scarlettine)

'No I don't, show-off.' (Me)

'When Great-Aunt Angria made a toast to you, I didn't drink. Did you, Frosty?'

'I most certainly did not.'

'We've seen you sucking up to her. I suppose you think you're her pet, as well as Grandma's.' (Scarlettine)

'You do, you know. You think you're great.' (Frostia)

'No I don't, big nose.'

'But you're not great. You're rubbish. And we're sleeping in your room!' (Scarlettine)

'Don't you dare! Hey, come back here! You *dare* pinch my room! You *dare* …'

And so on. It ended in a major fight, of course. It always does. I won't bore you with the details. If you've got sisters, you know how these things go. Instead, I'll tell you what happened to Uncle Bacchus. I'm sure you're dying to know. The story came out slowly over the next few days, so I'll sum it up for you.

Apparently, it was all down to a chapter of accidents. Uncle's castle is on the very edge of a cliff. One morning a week or so ago, he went out with a crate of empties and fell down the cliff on to the beach. When he came to, he had lost his memory, of all things! He spotted a rowing boat and, assuming he was a sailor, got in and put out to sea. There followed a series of adventures involving flying fish, mermaids and what have you. He finally got washed up on a strange shore, followed a signpost *To the Forest* and got mixed up in the wrong story.

It doesn't seem to have hurt him much. His memory came back once he started eating properly and everyone likes him with a beard.

Daddy was quite surprised when he arrived back to find us all home again. He gave us all a hug each, apart from Aunt Angry, whom he eyed with cold suspicion. However, later that day I heard him offering to give her a tour of his tomatoes, so I think they'll probably end up friends.

Mrs Pudding's celebration feast for Denzil doubled as a welcome home banquet for Aunt Angry. Nobody dared say we'd eaten already. Funnily enough, we all managed to do justice to it. Fairy food looks and tastes wonderful, but an hour or so later, you're starving again. The only person not present at the table was Alvis, who apparently was out spreading the new, superior mulch. As soon as I'd eaten my fill, I set off to find him.

He had finished gardening and was in his room, strumming his guitar. He was wearing his spangly jacket and tight trousers and blue shoes. Buster the dog was with him. So was Ralph. There's something about Alvis that attracts animals. They were both sitting adoringly at his feet, listening to him play.

'Hi, Wilma,' said Alvis, when I walked in. 'How's it goin'?'

'All right,' I said. 'Actually, I've been having quite an exciting time.'

'Yeah? Like, what?'

So I told him. I gave a long, detailed account of everything that had happened since we last saw each other. It took ages.

'Great!' said Alvis, when I finally ground to a halt. 'Hey! Sounds like you bin havin' fun.'

'What about you?' I asked. 'What have you been doing?'

'Spreading two tonnes of mulch for your dad.'

'No, I mean, before that.'

'Told you. I went fishin',' said Alvis.

'Catch any?'

'Yep. Threw 'em back, though.'

We sat in companionable silence for a while. Then I said:

'I've been practising C. I'm not sure I'm doing it right.'

He passed me his guitar.

'Let's hear it.'

I played it.

'Move your little finger to the next string up.'

'Like this?'

I tried. It came out sounding right this time.

'Cool,' said Alvis.

And together, we went back to join the party.

POSTSCRIPT

Just to bring you up to date, here are a few pieces of news:

1. *Beauty and Brett got married. None of us was invited to the wedding. But neither were the Good Fairies, so that was all right.*

2. *Scarlettine and Frostia are back at home, living with us while they get their silly lives sorted out. They're trying to get Mother to kick me out of my bedroom, but so far I'm managing to hang on in there.*

3. *Uncle Bacchus is living here too, for the time being. Mother thinks he needs feeding up.*

4. *Aunt Maud and New Uncle Frank have taken their caravan and gone off to a folk festival. They left in*

the middle of the night, so that they wouldn't have to take Grandma.

5. Aunt Angry is still here, on an extended visit. She seems to be enjoying herself. The other day, I got her to promise to release all those poor Enchanted ones from the Room of Living Statues, which is a result. Mrs Pudding has a sister who says she'll go and give Starkacre Hall a bit of a spring clean when she finally decides to return. So far, she and Grandma are getting on all right, although they go in for a lot of low-key bickering. Now I've got two old women going on at me.

6. Ralph is still here too. He follows Alvis around like a dog. I think he's trying to teach Buster to talk. No joy so far.

I started this account by saying that the letter from Aunt Angry changed my life. It did, too. I've got my work experience and will be taking my Grade Four Magic exam next week. There'll be no stopping me then. And I got in quite a bit of guitar practice. I've moved on to G now.

I would stop there, but there's one thing I'm sure you're dying to know. Did Daddy win first prize at the Tomato of the Year Show?

Well. He has four fully fledged wicked queens, two hippies, one wine god, one Faerie, Alvis and me on his side. What do you think?